ALSO BY MARK

One Night in Bridgeport

The Marfa Lights and Other Stories

Shady Acres and Other Stories

Deviation: A Long Short Story

The Irrepairable Past

The Dime

The Basement

You can follow me at:

www.markpaxson.com
www.kingmidgetramblings.wordpress.com
On Twitter: @mkpaxson
On Instagram: @mkpaxson

Slice of Life Stories - an occasionally updated podcast with stories and writing updates available on podcast platforms everywhere.

KILLING BERTHOLD GAMBREL

GAMBREL

A Collection

Mark Paxson

DEDICATION

To Berthold Gambrel, who was not killed as far as I know,
but who is undoubtedly one of the biggest supporters
of independent authors out there.

Note: This is a collection of short stories, interspersed with poems and pieces of flash fiction that have no titles. Most of these untitled pieces were the results of prompts. They're experiments, random pieces, and are included … well, just for the heck of it. Many of the pieces here were originally published on my blog, but there are a few pieces that have never before seen the light of day.

CONTENTS

Killing Berthold Gambrel

The first thing I need to say is that I never meant to do it. It was never ... NEVER ... my plan to see Berthold die. In fact, I wish he was still here, writing stories, short and long. Plying his craft in that half manic way all talented writers seem to do. I mean, seriously, the man has more talent behind his sparkling eyes and Cheshire grin than most of us wannabes can ever dream of.

Here's the second thing you should know. I didn't actually kill Berthold Gambrel. He did it by his own hand. People may argue, and that's probably why I'm sitting in the Mendocino County jail right now, that I provided him with the means to do it. That I might as well have pulled the trigger and put a bullet in his brain. But that would all be a pack of lies. For one thing, there wasn't a gun involved. For another, I wasn't even there when he died. I only arrived after his last breath, when the blood had stopped pooling.

To tell you the truth of the matter, I have to go back to the beginning. Okay. Maybe earlier. Before the beginning. I was at my local writing workshop. The leader spoke of Berthold Gambrel in such glowing terms and read excerpts from one of his novels. But, way before that, I was running in a marathon training group with a new friend. We found out we both wrote. Me, fiction. Him, poetry. Although he was beginning to dabble in short stories.

He – well, I guess he should have a name, otherwise you, the reader, may get lost. I mean so far, I've only named Berthold in this ramble of a story. You know nothing of me except that I sit in jail for his death. My workshop leader is not only nameless, but also sexless as well. And now, I've introduced a friend. You must want a name.

His name was ... well, wait a second, isn't that an odd thing about writing in the past tense? "His name was" suggests he is no more. He most definitely is still more. Unlike Berthold, who most definitely is now in the was category. His name is, most emphatically is, Rich. I met him on a training run.

1

Rich is one of those guys who knows every obscure writer there is. And he expected me to know them as well. If I write, I must be as literate as he is. Or is it was? He threw names out left and right and then would raise his eyebrows when I would shrug. So obscure I can't even remember the name of one of them to hold up and say "see, who ever heard of this guy?" Rich had, and he could quote the author and, well, here's what he could do.

We're ending a run and talking about writing and he says something like this, "Berthold Gambrel. You ever read him?" The eyebrows went up in tandem with my shoulders. "Well, he could do this thing …" And Rich would be off describing the thing. All of these writers he threw at me while I dodged my way through my apparently illiterate past always had a thing they did. What was Berthold's thing according to Rich? I can't possibly remember any more.

All I know is this. That was back before the beginning, before I ever knew I'd end up in the same room with Berthold Gambrel doing his thing.

I wonder what Rich thinks of me now. Caught after a high speed chase up Hwy 1 in the fog and dark of a late July evening. High speed there being 10 miles an hour on the hairpins and, because of the fog, 30 on the straightaways that last just long enough for the next breakneck curve to appear and slap you into your seat belt. They got me just before Westport. Three cops behind me. Two in front. You ever seen the flashing blues and reds in pea soup fog? You should. Just once. Hopefully, if you do, they won't be coming for you.

Could word have got to Rich already? Is he mourning the loss of a modern great one who had a thing like the dead guy? Well, wait a sec, I guess Berthold's a dead guy with a thing now, too. Maybe Rich would appreciate the cruel irony there. Isn't death what it takes for obscurity to become greatness?

That was before the beginning. Then there was the beginning. The workshop leader read an excerpt from *The Directorate*. She spoke glowingly of the book and of Berthold's storytelling ability. During a break, one of the workshop participants mentioned that the fabulous Mr. Gambrel would be leading a Short Fiction workshop at a writing conference in Mendocino. And I was off. The web gave me the details. I found a great place to stay. Added a couple of days on after the conference ended for some me time and made my plans.

I got into Berthold's Master Class on Short Fiction. Shocking, I know. They knew not what they were doing allowing a mere pretender such as myself into what I was sure would be an august group of writers. In preparation, I knew I needed to discover Berthold's genius before I arrived in Fort Bragg. I purchased the aforementioned *The Directorate* and *Vespasian Moon's Fabulous Autumn Carnival*. If I was going to be in a class with him for three days, I surely needed to read his works. To learn about him and how he wrote. To properly fawn over him in the quiet moments when I could gush over that thing he did on page 183 and how he wrapped it all up in the end.

Here's where the grand plan began to crash down upon me. I read *The Directorate*, but just barely, even if there was a space elevator in the story. After that slog, I moved on to something else that most definitely had nothing to do with Vespasian Moon. I arrived in Fort Bragg, as a result, completely unprepared for the fawning and gushing.

The conference and the morning workshop with Berthold came and went. The details of the workshop discussions are mostly irrelevant so I won't bore you with the details. For if I were to do so here, I might find it necessary to editorialize about the other participants. None of whom turned out to be scary like I thought they would be. We were all struggling writers reaching for the dream. Of various pedigrees and talents, we gathered and discussed.

No need to discuss such things as the fabulous Mr. Takei who spoke critically of other's failed efforts to connect with him emotionally but then defended his unemotional jaunt through extramarital affairs by stating, "I tend to write emotions very minimally." No need to discuss, the wonderful Scirocco Palomar who could never actually talk about the big picture of a story, but who demanded that every little thing must be explained. Every little nuance and allegation, hint and accusation, must not be left to the reader's imagination. The author must explain it all, fully and in detail.

No. I shant discuss those things here. I will also avoid my great displeasure that my story was taken up at the very end of the whole thing, leaving me guessing and wondering where I fit into it all.

Instead, I'll start where it began to get ugly. It was the local girl who started it. Bringing maple frosted cupcakes for everybody. Amily was her name. Yes, Amily. She was nice. Talkative as all get out. But a decent person. I mean who brings cupcakes for twelve mostly strangers who isn't nice. Some people picked at theirs. Oh, wait a sec, I think she even brought gluten-free cookies for the participants who were averse to gluten. See. She was that nice. Too damn nice.

So, that's the tally. I couldn't fawn or gush over his books. Although by the end of the workshop I had bought two more. Exactly what I needed. A library of books by an author whose style may not actually work for me. I cracked one of them open the last afternoon and started scanning the first story. *The Revival and Other Stories* – his first published work, award winning, critically acclaimed. And after a few pages I wondered if it would end up in the same category as *The Directorate*. Back to the tally. No fawning, no gushing. No cupcakes. Nothing other than my presence to impress this man who had the holy grail. An agent, a publisher, contracts, books published the traditional way. He had what I wanted.

The local girl though had an in. Cupcakes and jokes about giving him the poisoned one. Sure, build a rapport with him, while I could only sit on the sidelines and watch.

I got my chance, though, later. A few of us gathered at the Tip Top Lounge the final evening of the workshop. We had a couple of drinks, toasted each other, promised to keep in touch, and help each other out. I was getting up to leave and head back to my rental. I looked forward to the next couple of days when I could explore and be quiet again. All this interaction with strangers had worn me out.

That's when Gambrel came in. Damn, if the setting sun didn't create a halo around him. As I approached him, he smiled and dipped his head to me.

Amily saw him and screamed, "Berthold, over here." Gambrel looked at me again. I may have imagined it, it was hard to see his face in the darkened bar with the sun behind him, but I thought he raised his eyebrows at me. Like a pleading expression. "Save me," he seemed to be suggesting.

Save him? I turned back to the group. Four of our little gang of wannabe writers crowded around a high-top table. Amily, all bubbly … and fake. She was already walking towards Gambrel, trying to reel him in so she could be within his aura.

Robert, who said my story was about a social family, a concept I was still noodling over. It made it all sound so weighty, when all I wanted to do was write a story about three kids growing up in difficult times. And most importantly, write it from the shifting perspectives of each of those kids. I thought that could be my thing. Because after listening to my new friend Rich enough, I began to think every writer needs a thing.

Scirocco, still drinking the same glass of white wine. Rarely did she engage in conversation except when it turned to the writing itself. Her work far exceeded the rest of us. She already had a publisher. Why was she even there?

And Iris, the older lady whose story was about the gardener who worked on her flowers and reminded her of the man who took her virginity all those decades ago.

Takei had been there for a few moments, downing a beer – Pabst Blue Ribbon – before begging his pardon. I'm sure he was off in search of emotion and feeling.

Save him? Nah. "I guess I'm rejoining the party. What'll you have? It's on me." I took Gambrel by the elbow and steered him towards the table. After I ordered another beer for me and a whiskey on the rocks for him, I leaned over to Amily. "Let's get him drunk as shit." She giggled.

We did just that. Over the next two hours, I plied him with drinks. Iris fawned all over him, telling Gambrel how wonderful his books were and when he turned his attention to Amily or one of the others, I thought I saw a crazy little glint in her eye. Her brow would crinkle, her lips would tighten. Ah, Iris, all 60+ years of her, had a little bit of a crush on the man.

To be honest, who wouldn't? His dimpled chin, his neatly mussed hair, and that aw shucks sense of humor were all ... just right. And he had that thing we all wanted. He was published and reputable and critically acclaimed. But I wasn't crazy about him, like ol' Iris was. He seemed to be playing a role more than anything else. Charming author, leading all of us down the path towards the promised land.

Gambrel had a good word for each of us that night. He liked Amily's passion – Takei would probably disagree, believing her writing was utterly lacking in feeling. He respected Robert's use of the language – Takei would probably disagree, believing his writing didn't connect with the reader. Gambrel thought Scirocco had the most potential, that she had a gift of character – Takei would probably disagree, concluding her characters were too flat.

For me, after one or two more whiskeys, Gambrel simply said, "I like that you use different voices."

5

"Thanks," I replied. "I was just experimenting. Trying to come up with a different way to tell a story."

"Yes, that's it." He slapped his hand down on the table. "Experiment. Push the envelope. Keep working on this story. I'd like to see what you do with it."

Takei would have said … well, who the hell cares about Takei? He wasn't there anymore, the workshop was over. Takei had probably returned home to his cold, barren flat in San Francisco and his cat. I'd never talk to him again.

At some point crazy ol' Iris left. Maybe she realized Gambrel had nothing for her. She hardly said a word when she walked out. She was there and then she was gone.

Robert left shortly after. "My wife is waiting up for me, I'm sure," he sighed. "It's time for me to get back home."

"You're a good man," Gambrel slurred while he rose from a stool to shake Robert's hand. "He's a good man, right? Amily?"

While they discussed the goodness of Robert, a topic I cared nothing about, I ordered another drink for Gambrel. When the waitress set it in front of him, I asked, "What's your thing, Berthold?"

He took a sip of his new drink, burped, and asked, "What do you mean?"

"You know. Your stories. How do you do it?" I took my own sip, from a beer I'd been nursing for more than an hour. "They're so random, disorganized almost. I don't get it."

"You should."

"Huh?"

"Of everybody in this group, you should get it. You're the one that's trying to do something different."

"Yeah, but that's not the same. I'm just trying different voices, you're … you're …" I finished my beer and watched him down a big gulp of his whiskey. "You do something I just can't figure out."

Before Gambrel could reply, Amily put her hand on my arm and stopped me. "Why do you think there's something to figure out?"

"I … I … because …," I sputtered. "Have you read his stories? He does something and I can't make sense of it. They're disconnected but suggest something more."

Berthold just smiled. "A writer never shares his secrets."

"Whatever," I muttered, choosing to focus on the dregs that remained in my glass. I downed the last drops and left the bar, leaving Amily and Gambrel behind.

It was only an hour or so after I left when my phone started vibrating on the nightstand. I considered ignoring it. Even more so when I didn't recognize the number, but the area code was local. I accepted the call. I wish I hadn't. Of everything that happened that night, taking the call is the decision I wish I could go back to and change. I should have turned my phone off. Gone to sleep. In the morning, I would have been able to travel the coast and take pictures of the waves. Maybe hit the lighthouse south of town. Have some pizza and beer and do it all over again the next day. Until I had to return home.

"Hello?"

"It's Amily. You have to come. Quick. There's been an accident." She was breathless and talking so fast I could barely understand her and then she said something I heard loud and clear. "I think Berthold's dead."

"What? Wait?"

"You need to come. My parents can't know I … just come, Saul. Please."

"You think a man is dead and you're worried about your parents."

"Pleeeeease."

And I then made the second decision of the night I would regret later. I got in my car and drove out to Highway 1, turned north and found the wreck not too far down the road. What I should have done is reject Amily's pleas. After all, she had rejected my advances. I owed her nothing.

Yes, just before I tried to make my leave and then Gambrel showed up, I hit on her. Hard. Asked her back to the little cabin I was staying in. Told her about the little Zen garden that surrounded the cabin. Tried to make a joke about it, while meaning it entirely. I hated myself the entire time, the words coming out of my mouth while I desperately tried to stop them. I mean, there were the gluten-free cookies, and those stupid

7

cupcakes, and she was bubbly. I hated bubbly. This wasn't right. But I did it anyway and she shot me down without hesitation.

I had every right to reject Amily's request, but I didn't. In the dark and damp, the flashers on his car cast a blinking yellow pall in the fog that lay low that night. Amily stood outside the car, a bit of blood dripping down from a cut on her forehead. Gambrel, on the other hand, was crumpled against the steering wheel, with a whole lot of blood everywhere. His eyes were open, glassy and vacant.

I turned to Amily. "What happened?"

"He just crashed." She shrugged. "Probably had too much to drink."

"No shit. Why did you let him drive?"

"I had a lot, too." Amily closed the gap between us. "My parents will kill me if they find out about this. They still think I'm their little girl. No booze. No sex. No …"

"You're kidding me, right? How old are you? 28? 30?"

"Yes. I know. But I still live at home and, well … it's a small town. This would not look good."

And then I made my third bad decision of the night. "Go. Get out of here. Take my car. I'll deal with this." I just wanted her away from me.

The cops showed up a little while later. They asked me some questions and then let me go with a suggestion I not leave town for a few days "just in case."

"No plans to, Officer," I said. "At least not until Saturday or Sunday."

"Well, why don't you check in with us before you do?"

"Of course."

It may have been July, but at 1:00 in the morning, with fog shrouding the area, a damp deep cold had settled in. I burrowed into my jacket and walked the mile and a half back to my cabin.

Two days later, I was coming back from Mendocino. The sun had set, the fog rolled in. It was dark and I was inching along Highway 1 just north of Fort Bragg when the lights went on behind me. I panicked and kept driving as fast as the fog allowed me.

I guess that suggests guilt to any red-blooded cop, but what had I done? Nothing. Except for have a few drinks in Mendocino while I

8

watched the blue sky turn to orange and purple and then to black. Maybe I could lose them in the fog. Maybe that was the best sign of all that I probably had too much to drink.

They put me in cuffs without saying much except for reading me my Miranda rights. No walking a straight line, heel to toe. No backwards alphabet. Just the cuffs, my rights, and the backseat of the car. It wasn't until we got to the police station and a detective let the cat out of the bag. "You've been arrested in connection with the death of Berthold Gambrel, Mr. Rivers."

"What? WHAT? What the hell are you talking about? This isn't about …" Well, I just shut my mouth then. No sense in admitting I'd been driving drunk as well. "I think I need an attorney."

"You asking for an attorney?"

"I don't know. Yeah, I guess so."

"You sure you don't want to talk to me first," Detective Roth suggested. "Maybe we could resolve this and get you out of here."

It sounded attractive and I knew I had nothing to do with Gambrel's death. But they seemed to have some information that suggested I had killed the man. Amily!

There would be no sense in talking that night. "No. I've done nothing wrong, but I want to talk to an attorney first."

The detective tossed his pen on the table, shuffled some papers and closed his file. "Fine."

I knew a guy who knew a guy who answered phones for a criminal attorney. I called my friend and a day later the attorney called me. He was nearing the end of a trial, but he said he could get up to Fort Bragg in a couple of days. I told Roth. "Hey, no skin off my nose," he said. "Hearing is in a couple of days. Bail. A few other things. If you want to sit in a cell and eat jail food, that's on you."

So, I sat. And a day passed. And another.

"You've got a visitor," a guard told me as he opened the door to my cell. I had no idea who it could be. Joe Scheck, my attorney – a phrase I never thought I'd use - wasn't due until the next day when he would arrive and represent me at my arraignment and bail hearing. I had no idea who would have cared enough to visit.

9

Amily?!?! Would she? I relished the thought. I'd give her a piece of my mind, but first I'd grill her on what she told the cops. All the time sitting in a jail cell had given me plenty of time to figure out why the cops would think I had murdered Gambrel. It was her. That bitch. Amily.

It wasn't Amily. When I walked into the visiting room, I looked for her and found Iris. I looked around to make sure I wasn't missing something, wondered if maybe somebody was playing a joke on me, and when I realized there was nobody else there, I sat across the table from little old Iris. "Thanks for coming," I started, "but, what …"

"Stop. Listen to me. You need to understand this is bigger than you." Iris looked at me, her upper lip quivering, her fingers tapping a rapid, rhythmic beat on the table. "Have you ever heard of the Trilateral Commission? The Masonites? It's all connected you know. It's a conspiracy. Berthold was just an innocent victim, a pawn, and now," she almost looked like she was going to start crying. "you, you poor sweet man. You're caught up in it too.'

"What the hell are you talking about?"

"Ssssshh. It's time somebody did something about this. Blow the lid off what the powerful are doing. Shed a little light on matters. It's time for transparency and accountability." Iris actually reached her hand out and patted my arm. "Don't you think?"

I didn't know what to think. I had no idea what she was talking about, but I had a new sense of Iris. She was crazy as crazy can be. I laughed and pushed away from the table.

"Listen to me." Iris looked around and spotted a sheriff standing at the door. She smiled at him and gave a little fingertip wave. Turning back to me, the smile was gone and there was a steely fire in her eyes. "This is no laughing matter."

"But why would they care about me?" I couldn't help it. I had to see just how far she would go with this.

"They don't care about you. You're just collateral damage. Berthold, though, he was figuring it out." Iris stopped and began twirling a strand of hair while looking at me. "You didn't read *The Revival*, did you?"

"Uh, no. I mean, I started but I just couldn't get through it."

"Of course you didn't." Iris smiled at me then like she was humoring a small child. "It's all in there. Berthold revealed their secrets."

10

"Whose secrets?"

Iris picked up her purse and stood up. "You can't be that naïve, can you? I don't think I'm going to be able to help you. I just hope you take this seriously. You're probably next."

"What the hell are you . . ."

But she was gone before I could finish the question.

In the hours that followed, I was pulled out of my cell for more visitors. Each time, I hoped for my attorney. Each time, it wasn't.

First, it was Scirocco, who had just one question for me. "Why? Why did you do it? I need to understand your motivation?"

"I didn't do anything," I replied. "I didn't kill him."

"No, no, now. Tell me what happened. Step by step. I need to know."

I motioned to the guard. "I'm done here, take me back to my cell."

An hour later it was Takei, who drove up from San Francisco just to say, "What passion! What commitment! I knew you had it in you. Now, just put that in a story." Before I could respond, he was up and gone.

Robert, of course, was next, to tell me he knew there was a connection between Gambrel and me. He didn't think it would turn so dark, so quickly. He expressed his dismay and wished me "the best."

I sighed and returned to my cell.

Amily did not join the parade. Of course she didn't. I had no doubt she was staying as far away from law enforcement as she could.

She made an appearance anyway. First thing the next morning, a guard delivered a pink box – like you get at a donut shop. I knew what was inside before I opened it. Maple frosted cupcakes. Four of them. Before I could even think about what I was doing, I screamed, "Fuckin' Amily," and threw the box against the wall.

The guard turned back to me, eyebrows raised. I motioned him away. "No problem here," I said, as I leaned down to clean up the mess.

I finally met my attorney when I was escorted into the courtroom a couple of hours later. "Joe Scheck," he said, holding out his hand.

Before I could respond, the bailiff stood and called the courtroom to order, "The Honorable Wally Berger presiding."

We all stood. We all sat down and waited for the judge to shuffle some papers. When he was done, he looked around the courtroom and then at his clerk. "What do we have first, Lucinda?"

"People v. Rivers, your Honor." She handed him a file.

The judge looked at the file and then to the district attorney. "What's your argument on bail?"

"Mr. Rivers has been charged with murder. We admit it's an odd case, but we believe he set out to kill Mr. Gambrel intentionally. A crime of jealousy."

"Gambrel?" Judge Berger mused. "Why does that name sound familiar?"

"He's an author," the prosecutor replied. "He was here for the writer's conference."

The judge looked over at me. "Berthold Gambrel, the author of *The Directorate*, that Gambrel?"

"Yes," the prosecutor said. "The one and only."

Judge Berger slammed his hand down on his desk. Then he grabbed his gavel and slammed that down. "You killed Berthold Gambrel?!'

"I didn't," I yelled back. My attorney tried to shut me up, but I got the words out before he could.

"Your honor," Scheck began, before the judge continued.

"The author of *The Directorate*, the creator of the space elevator. A genius of fiction and of science fiction. You killed him?!"

"I ...," this time, Scheck put his hand over my mouth and what I said after that was a muffled word salad.

"Your honor, my client will be pleading innocent when the time is right. I thought we were here to talk about bail and to enter that plea."

Judge Wally Berger looked at his desk and at the file that was in front of him. He opened it, leafed through the pages and then closed the file again. We waited. He looked at me. "I think I've heard enough."

"What do you mean?" Scheck said. "I haven't had a chance to argue ... the prosecutor hasn't even finished his position on bail. What?"

"Mr. Gambrel did this thing in *The Directorate*. It was magical. It was ... I hate to repeat myself, but ... a space elevator."

I couldn't take it anymore. I pushed Scheck away from me and took a step towards the judge. "A thing? You call that a thing. A frickin' space elevator. That's a thing to you? Really?" Scheck tried to stop me, but I ignored him. "That's not a thing. That's just ... I mean, what even is a space elevator? How does it work? Where does it go?" I looked at him, amazed that I was even having this argument with a judge while I stood accused of murder. "It's not actually a thing."

"Says you," the judge said. "I say otherwise and ... I ...," he reached for his gavel, "I ... I find you guilty!" He slammed his gavel down so hard it shattered.

Scheck started yelling. The prosecutor sat down with a puzzled look on his face. And I looked around just as flummoxed.

"Bailiff, take him away," the judge ordered. "Lock him up! LOCK HIM UP!"

The judge rose and turned with a twirl of his robe and exited he courtroom through the door to his chambers.

"What just happened?" I asked Scheck.

"I don't know. Apparently, this Gambrel fella had a thing," he shrugged. "I guess I'm gonna have to read *The Directorate* now."

Where This Came From: A number of years ago, I attended a writers' conference in Fort Bragg, one of my most favorite places in the world. There was a morning session much like what is described in this story. But Berthold did not lead that group. No, he wasn't anywhere close. Afterwards, a couple of the participants kept in touch via email and I made a comment that I wanted to write a story like this about the real author who led the group. The idea being nothing other than a story entitled "Killing XXXX XXXX." And here it is. I didn't get the author's permission to use his name, but Berthold volunteered to be the subject of this story. How could I resist? By the way, Berthold isn't actually dead. He's alive and well, planning more stories with space elevators. Hopefully.

* * * * *

Hello to you, my friend
For hours, we sit at this place
Our words filling the space
I hope I've helped you mend

Go out, take care, be you.
Pick up the pieces
Life never ceases
Good-bye until tomorrow, it's brand new

Carnies

The echoes of children giggling, mothers yelling, and men boasting still reverberated along the midway. A full moon hung without a net in the sky above the Ferris Wheel. The ground was tacky with spilled sodas and ice cream splatters. My nostrils were filled with the odor of popcorn and the vomit left behind by the punk coming off the tilt-a-whirl with a shit-eating grin on his face, convinced he was gonna knock down the bottles until his stomach started to rumble.

"Sallie, let me get that for you."

I leaned against the booth's frame. "Thanks, Buck. It's like an ice pick borin' a hole in me tonight." I massaged the small of my back and then reached out to pat him on the shoulder as he reached up to bring the door down, the clanging rattle of the door on its tracks getting slammed to the ground chasing away the last echoes of the day, and the quiet of the midway late at night overwhelmed me like it did most nights. Most everybody else had finished up, cleaned up, locked up and returned to their trailers in the boneyard, tucked away in the far corner of the parking lot, where I had a bed and a locker in the bunkhouse.

"Why they call you Sallie?" Buck asked, snapping the lock shut on my booth.

I sighed and looked over his shoulder at the shuttered midway. The flashing lights were off, the stuffed animals stowed away. This was my time. I could shuffle my old bones through the games and rides and remember …

… The Griswold Traveling Carnival. I was fourteen when I ran away. Ol' man Griswold took me under his wing.

… The Elastic Girl, who just so happened to be my first. And Griswold's daughter. And the reason I had to run away from the Griswold Traveling Carnival when I was sixteen.

"I mean, you an old white man. It's not like you a girl or nothing like that." Buck paused for a moment. I tried to laugh him off. It didn't work. "You ain't a girl, right?"

Apparently, I wouldn't get the quiet I wanted.

"Why Sallie?" I muttered at Buck as I began to walk and motioned for him to follow. "Well, that's a story we may not have time for." I thought for a moment I might stall him. He was a 24-hour man and with the joint breaking down soon, he'd be gone in the morning, scouting out our next stop. We were barnstorming that summer and Buck had to get on down the road.

"Hell, at your pace, it mighta be a week 'fore we get to the trailers." Buck took a flask from a pocket and took a swig. "Whassa story?"

I noted he did not offer the flask to me and silently thanked Buck for that. Maybe he knew. It was always hard to know, in the little world of a traveling show, what people knew. Stories were told. Rumors shared. Maybe he knew I was on the wagon. At least for that day, I was. The problem was … there was no story to tell. I was born. I had a name. What it was didn't matter. When I hit the road, somebody called me Sallie. And it stuck.

But sometimes, you know, you gotta tell a story. Buck and I, we were walking by the concession stands, where the smell of cotton candy and corn dogs and stale popcorn had stayed strong. Next up was the chump twister and a row of apple joints. Shuttered for the night. Quiet, except for the echoes that rang in my head of the carnies spinning their lines.

… Old man Griswold, I told him it was the boys on my street who came up with it. That's all he needed to hear.

… And later on and further down the road, when I told a girl it was my momma's name and when she died, I took as my own and that got me a whole lot of everything.

… And the truth.

That it was the Elastic Girl who called me Sallie one night when we were in her trailer because when you're the daughter of the owner you get a trailer to yourself instead of a broken down cot in the bunkhouse – which is nothing more than an 18-wheeler pulled up besides the trailers – not that I was complaining because it was the trailer that provided the place where I discovered the things that men need to know.

The haunted house came up on our left. On our right, a coin toss game. Up ahead, the moon had dropped a bit, just touching the upper edge of the ferris wheel. And Buck waited while we walked.

"Her name was Katie."

"Yeah? Who?"

"She was the Elastic Girl at the first joint I worked. She said I wasn't no rube. Or a clem. Or chump. No, Katie said there was something about me that she saw. I was a bit stronger." We approached the arch at the entrance to the show. The empty parking lot awaited us. "She said she didn't know a guy like me. 'You can take a name like Sallie, can't you?' she said. I remember this, we were in her bed with the sheets wrapped around us. I was teasing her nipple with my finger. I'da 'greed with just about anything she said at that moment.

"The next day, I was walking to my game – I was operating a cheese wheel, 'cause it was all ol' Griswold thought I could handle – when one of the freaks called out, 'Hey Sallie, my boy.'"

Buck stopped. "You shittin' me, man?"

"No. I learned something that day."

"Whassat?"

"The freaks … they stick together."

* * * * *

The thing was this. I wasn't gonna have no damn mulatto baby running around my carnival. It made no never mind to me that the boy was sprinklin' the sheets with Katie. Long as he kept it straight during the day, it made no difference to me how bent he got at night or if he won the bedroom bingo with my girl. If the carnies worked hard in the light of day, they went harder at it at night. I knew this when I brought Katie to the bus'ness. I'm sure the boy wasn't her first, even if'n he turned out to be her last. She was a thing I had to give up.

I needed her to make the whole thing go. A black man in the white man's world in the '50's was nothin' more than a nigga. Hell, the white folk didn't even know the traveling show was mine. Griswold was long dead. Knifed in his sleep. Mornin after, I stood forward. Carnies didn't care my color or nothin' else other than were their envelope gonna have somethin' in it come Friday morning. And if the kid and other newbies thought I was Griswold, it all worked for me.

18

The Elastic Girl did things that made the white ladies gasp, but I knew this. While their women were shocked, the white men were thinkin' only one thing. That's what kept the tent full and allowed me to charge an extra two bits for her show. I seen it in the shine of their eyes and the way their mouths hung open. Those men, who thought nothin' of sayin', "out of the way, ya nigger," when they hustled out of the tent and brushed past me, couldn't take their eyes off'n my Katie. As black as the night she was, but there are certain things that no skin color gonna matter. And one of 'em is men and they cocks. I saw in their eyes their dreams of havin' her legs wrapped aroun' their hips while they did the boogie-woogie. I'm sure a few of 'em wouldn'ta minded seein' Katie in a good ol' cootch show, but I had my limits. Asides, I'da lost the payin' ladies if I put her in a cootch show.

So, yeah, I used my Katie, but I was always there. Watchin'. Makin' sure none of the crackers got outta hand and when her show was over, I let my girl do whatever. I owed her that, dint I?

The best part 'bout those days was the special shows we put on for the black folk. Nary but a few of 'em could scrape together enough jangling coins or crumpled bills to enter. We did 'em one better tho'. A free show our first night in town. Five or ten miles outta on some ol' uncle's pasture so the white folk didn't know, we'd put up one tent and give 'em a show. A whole lot of hootin' and hollerin', singin' and dancin', we'd do whateva' come to mind. Maybe even in the wee hours of the night give 'em a little bit of the scramble egg treatment.

My carnies didn't care. Besides what twas in their envelope, they cared about havin' fun. Rippin' it up and tearin' it down wheneva' they had the chance. Those shows for the negroes, well, those were what the carnies woulda done if they could. Each and every day. So help me, that's the Lord's truth.

So, ya gotta see it my way. Things were in a balance and goin' good. If it kept on keepin' on, I mighta been able to roll up the tents for good, find misself a little spot o' land back home in Georgia and stop the travelin'. I'da be able to keep Katie there, too, among her own folk. Mebbe I'd no longa see the sparklin' eyes of all those white men in my dreams anymore.

The boy, Sallie, tol' me a story. A bunch o' cock and bull 'twas. One day, I hear a man call him Sallie and I pult him to me. "Wassup with that?" I ask. "Why you let him call you Sallie? You tol' me your name was Frank."

The way he looked at me, I knew sumtin' was up. "Ah, it's nothing," he say.

"Nuthin'." I stepped back from him. "You almost a man now, you can't be lettin' 'em call you Sallie."

"It's no problem at all," he say again. "Just a name I picked up on the rails. An ol' blind tramp called me it. I told one of the fellas and I guess they just call me it for fun."

"Well, you oughta stick up for yaself."

I went on my way, puzzlin' in my head why a boy would let that happen and why this boy wouldn'ta look me in the eye. I liked the kid. What little he told me, his Pa was a hard one, who thought nothin' of bein' even harder on his own kin. I wanted to give him a chance. But I din't like the way he scurried away that mornin'.

I's slow, but I put it together when Katie came to me one mornin'.

"Papa?"

"Yeah, baby." I smiled at her. Couldn't help it, she just was my sunshine.

"I gots somethin' to tell you." She hesitated. "I is scared to, though."

"Well, you just tell me. No reason to be scart."

"Papa. I think I'm with child."

"You what?!" I had no right, truth be told. I know'd what was goin' on. Shit on the shock. I laid it out for her. "It's that boy, idn't it?"

"Y-y-y-esss," Katie stuttered out.

"Well, we'll jus' have to take care of it."

You see, a mulatto baby runnin' 'round, pullin' at Katie's skirts would mean too many questions. Who the father? Too many crackers coulda done it and I had no mind that the boy would stand up. Asides, I couldn't have no pregnant Elastic Girl. Afore Katie had a chance to say yay or nay, I went into town and found the white doc. Paid him good money to have the thing taken out of her.

And if that was all, I'd have let the boy alone. The thing was this. That night, I found my Katie in the donniker, all bled out. Yeah, the boy had to run agin.

20

Where This Came From: To be honest, I'm not entirely sure. It may have been. a story I worked on via an on-line workshop years ago. It may not be. I do know that, while I this works as a stand-alone story, it is also a part of something bigger I hope to get to at some point.

* * * * *

She wasn't beautiful, she knew that. But when she put on the mask and leapt out into the night, she felt like the scars of her past melted away. The first scar formed when her dad poked her in the stomach. "You're getting fat," he grumbled. She wasn't. She was five pounds underweight. But this is what he did. Relentlessly.

The second scar formed when her high school boyfriend forced her to have sex with him in the back seat of her car. She tried to stop him, but she couldn't. She wasn't strong enough. The next day he walked by her at school without saying a word. He texted her that night. "You're too skinny," was all it said.

The third scar was not one, but more than one. She started cutting herself. There were barely visible lattices of white lines that criss-crossed her thighs.

But with the mask on, nobody could see her scars. The doubt. The insecurity. What they saw instead was a confident woman who strode forward, commanding attention, while inside she felt like a child, still learning for her father's affection. A woman who wanted a lover. To never hurt herself again.

Some days were better than others.

What Happens When A Pet Dies

"What should we do with the body?"

"I don't know. It's too big to flush down the toilet. Remember when we flushed my goldfish when I was a kid? The mouse, too."

"You flushed the mouse down the toilet?"

"Sure. It was a little guy ..."

"Do you remember what you named the fish?"

"Yeah. Goldie?"

"Wow, that's some creative shit, right there. What did you name the mouse? I forgot."

"Little Guy."

"Even more creative." Bob, my brother, shook his head. "You never were the smartest one in the bunch."

"So what." I looked down at GP's corpse. "You got the creativity. You can paint and write and have that damn voice of yours. But I got the athletic talent, the physical prowess ... I mean, you couldn't even hit one of those bowls with a ping pong ball let alone actually get the ball inside one."

"Woohoo. Sparky has talent because he got a goldfish at the county fair."

"It's not just that, you know. You never made it out of right field when we played baseball, or got off the bench in football." I took my eyes off the dead animal and glanced at Bob. "Besides, what's all that creativity got for you. You work at Chili's, for christsake."

"You just wait." Bob started to wrap GP in a stained dish towel. "I'm gonna try out for American Idol next year and write a book about it. You'll see!"

"Sure you are." I laughed, hoping that Bob would laugh with me. "Just like I'm going to be playing first base for the Cubbies next year. Maybe you can write a book about that."

He didn't laugh. "Whatever." GP was fully wrapped in the towel. "So what are we going to do?"

"We can bury it."

"Where? There's no backyard here. We live in a frickin' apartment. Haven't you noticed there's nothing but concrete."

"Mom and Dad's?"

"No way. I'm not going over there." Bob shook his head. "Have you forgotten what happened the last time we were there?"

"No. I haven't. But maybe it's time."

"Nope. Not gonna happen. Dad gets drunk, he yells at me, makes me feel worthless, calls me a pansy and you and Mom just sit there. You want to go and bury your god-damn guinea pig, you go right ahead."

"Well, hell, if you're not going, I'm not either."

We stood quietly looking at GP, yes, my guinea pig named GP. Bob wasn't wrong about my lack of creativity. But then, you don't need creativity to be able to hit a curve ball or to make a three-point shot. You just need to block everything out of your head and focus on a single spot. That's what I'd been doing for years.

"Hey, I know," Bob said. "Don't they consider guinea pig a delicacy in Bolivia?"

"I think that's Peru."

"Nope. It's Bolivia. I'm sure of it."

"It's Peru. Or Argentina. But it's not Bolivia." I thought for a second. "I remember this ... uh ... Bolivia ... they're all about llama jerky."

"Llama jerky? You mean like beef jerky, but with llama?"

"Yep. Llamas, not guinea pigs."

"Huh. Llama jerky. I'll be damned."

We stood quietly some more, pondering the mystery of what to do with a dead guinea pig. "What were you going to do?" I finally asked. "Send it to some poor family in Bolivia for their Sunday meal?"

A dark look passed over Bob's face. "Nah. What do you think I am? An idiot?"

"Well ..."

24

"No. I wasn't thinking we could send it to Bolivia." He paused for a second, tried to smile, but failed, choosing to shrug instead. "I was thinking we could look up a recipe for guinea pig and see if it's any good."

"What the hell are you talking about?" I picked up GP and took a step back. "Let me repeat myself – what the hell?!"

"It was a joke, Sparky, just a joke." Bob sat down at the kitchen table we had been standing around. "Relax a bit. That's one of your problems. You're too serious."

"You just suggested eating my guinea pig, and I'm the one with the problem?"

"Fine. I'm sorry. I am really sorry that I made a tasteless joke." He held his hands out and dipped his head to me. "Now, sit down."

I did. "What are we going to do?" I asked.

"There's the dumpster out back."

"True." He had a point. The dumpster was probably the only option, but it hardly seemed dignified at all. Goldie got a burial at sea. Sort of. When our dog died, Dad in between drinking jags, dug a hole and we buried Speckles under the peach tree. We always said things when we buried our pets. "But I can't see just throwing GP into the dumpster. We need to say something, don't we?"

"What, some kind of 'dearly departed' prayer or something?" Now he did laugh. "You're not exactly the religious type, you know."

"So ..."

"Hold on a sec," Bob said, interrupting me. "It's a god-damn guinea pig, Sparky. A ... guinea ... pig. Come on, just find a shoe box, tape it shut, and let's go throw it in the dumpster."

He had a point. Maybe I was just tired. "Okay. Let's do it," I said as tears started to well up. I sniffed.

"You're not crying, are you?"

"Just a bit."

"My God, crying over ..."

"Stop it, would you. Can you just let me this one time feel what I'm feeling and not knock me for it? Just this once? Can you do that?"

25

"Fine." Bob remained quiet while I wiped my eyes and took a couple of deep breaths. "You ready?"

"I guess."

Bob went into his bedroom and came back with the required shoe box. Nike, of course. I gently placed GP into the box and put the lid on. Bob wrapped tape around it a few times to make sure it stayed closed and off we went.

It was when we turned the corner of our apartment building and I saw the dumpster when I realized I couldn't do it. "Bob?" I stopped walking. He took a couple more steps before turning back to me.

"What now?"

"I can't … I can't throw him into a dumpster." I pointed at the rusting piece of metal with piles of garbage spilling out. "I mean … look at it. I'm not going to just toss GP in there and walk away." I turned around and started walking back to our apartment. "No, I'm not."

"Sparky. Come on." Bob got ahead of me and turned around, holding his hands out to stop my forward movement. "It's just a guinea pig."

"To you." I brushed past him and kept going.

"What are you going to do then?"

"Mom and Dad's."

"Aah, man."

"You don't need to come with me." I looked back at Bob as I started to climb the stairs to our apartment. "Dad might call you a pansy again."

"I'm going."

"Whatever. Do what you want."

In the apartment, I grabbed my car keys. Bob joined me as I walked to my car. Once inside, I handed him the shoe box. We sat quietly on the drive to our parents' home. The place we grew up. Where things happened. Where sometimes the sun shone and other times it was a dark, dark place. We could only wonder what we would find when we got there.

When I pulled up in front of their house, Bob broke the silence. "How long has it been?"

I thought about it. I remembered being there for Mom's 60th birthday. It was a hot June day. But I couldn't think of any time since then that we had seen our parents. "I don't know. A couple of years maybe?"

"Yeah. I think you're right." We sat in the car for a moment. "You ever call them? Either one?"

"I talk to Mom every now and then. You?"

"Same."

Bob heaved a sigh and opened his door. "Let's go. Let's get this done. Bury your damn guinea pig and get a beer."

"You buying?"

"Sure. If that's what it takes to get this over with."

We walked to their front door. Bob knocked. Mom opened the door. Her eyes lit up. "Boys!!"

"Hey Mom," we said simultaneously.

"Come in, come in."

It was hard not to feel the infectious quality of our mother's happiness that we were there. Maybe this was going to be okay. "Dad around?" I asked as we entered our childhood home.

"Oh. I'm sure he's around somewhere. Don't know where." She giggled quietly, averted her eyes from us, and ushered us into the family room. "It's been so long. I'm so happy to see both of you. My boys."

Inside, nothing had changed. Mom had the family room furniture in the summer layout, with nothing blocking the sliding glass door to the backyard. The kitchen was spotless. There was a puzzle at one end of the dining room table.

"What's in the box?" Mom asked.

"GP."

"GP?"

"His guinea pig, Mom," Bob said. "It's dead. We came here to bury it."

"Oh my." Mom put her hand to her mouth. "Are you okay?"

Before I could reply, Bob did. "Of course he is. It's a damn guinea pig."

27

"Shut up," I said through gritted teeth. "Just shut up."

Bob sighed. "Whatever," he mumbled before starting to walk towards the sliding glass door. "We thought he could bury it in the back where Speckles is."

"Well, sure." Mom started walking towards the door to the garage. "I'll get you boys a shovel." She stopped and turned back to us. "Will you stay for dinner?"

"Of course," I replied, looking at Bob who had turned to me, quietly shaking his head back and forth. "Right, Bob?" He shook his head one last time and resumed his walk towards the backyard and the shady corner under the tree where our childhood dog was resting in peace.

I followed behind Bob, with the box held in front of me. When Bob opened the sliding glass door and walked through, I heard him grunt, saw him slow to a stop. "Hey, Pops," he said through what sounded to me like a clenched jaw.

"Bob? Charlie?"

"Hey, Dad," I said.

"Well, isn't this a nice surprise?" Dad got up from his lounger, stumbled for a moment before righting himself. Behind him, I could see the small accumulation of beer cans on the table he kept next to the chair, along with a cheap paperback and a pack of cigarettes. Before he continued, he belched for good measure. "To what do I owe this pleasure? My boys paying a visit after, what, how long has it been?" He yawned, scratched his growing belly, and picked up a beer. "Cheers," he said as he brought it to his mouth and guzzled from it.

He was like a pig at a trough. Slurping and burping, and generally not caring about anything other than what was in his trough. Beer. Glorious, wonderful beer. It was pretty much how he'd gone through his entire life, or at least the part I was aware of. His wife was his slop-tender, pushed out of the way as soon as food was on his plate, or beer was put in front of him. From what I heard, it was the same way where he worked. Just a ravenous glutton unaware of others.

"Cheers," I said. "Ummm … my guinea pig died. We were going to bury him back in the corner. Under the tree."

"Well, isn't that just too damn cute?" He turned to Bob then, looked him up and down. "And you, you're along for the ride on this one? Of course, you are. You're still soft, aintcha."

"I knew we shouldn't have come here," Bob said.

"Dad, knock it off," I said to him. "Bob didn't want to do this. It was my idea. I couldn't throw GP into the dumpster. You wanna call somebody soft, talk to me. I'm the soft one."

He looked back and forth between us, took another gulp out of his beer. "Hell, what did I ever do to deserve two weak-ass sons? You played sports. I took you to games. I taught you how to be men. And look at you now. Burying your stupid little guinea pig and your big brother is here, too. What are you, Bob, his support system? Hell."

Bob started walking towards our father. The look on his face told me that he intended on showing our dear old dad exactly what he was. I stepped between the two of them, placing the box that held GP on the table we used to eat at for summer barbecues. "Stop." I placed my hands on Bob's chest and gently pushed him. "Stop," I repeated.

He didn't. He pushed into me. His eyes unfocused. His mouth clenched.

"Stop," I said again. Louder. And I pushed him back harder. "Bob. Go inside with Mom." I realized then that Mom had never come out with the shovel. I had a feeling I knew why. She knew that nothing good would come of this and decided to hide herself away. If she didn't see it. If she didn't hear it. Maybe it never happened.

"Screw it," Bob spat at me. "I'm gone. This was a stupid idea. We should have never come here."

Bob walked back through the sliding glass door with me in close pursuit. "Bob, come on. Let's just get this done. Ignore him. Can't you do that?"

"Nope. Not gonna happen. I'm outta here."

What could I do? He was my ride home. I followed him out to the car. It was only when we were out of the neighborhood and halfway to our apartment that I realized something. "Dammit. I left GP there."

"Too bad. So Sad."

Where This Came From: This story was written to submit to The First Line, a quarterly journal where each story in an issue begins with the same first line. My story wasn't accepted, so here it is.

* * * * *

It goes like this, you see. Life is like having a butterfly on your nose. You know it could be beautiful, but you just can't quite focus on it because your eyes cross when you try. So you're not entirely sure.

You want to shake it off, but then it might fly away and then where would you be. You wouldn't have the beauty you think exists anymore. So, you try to stay as still as possible. If you're quiet, the butterfly will stay. If you're quiet, your life will be good. Trouble might pass you by. If you stay still, trauma and drama will pass over you.

But the butterfly on your nose is starting to tickle. You want to twitch your nose, rub the tip with your finger. Maybe if you could, reach your tongue up there and lick the itch away.

What do you do? Stay still and be quiet, let the beauty remain even if you can't quite see it. Do you let the minor discomfort of the tickle disrupt things? Maybe if you did, once the butterfly leaves, two more would appear. Or a slug.

What do you do?

Nobody Important

I was sitting in a room. A single light bulb in the center of the ceiling lit the space. I was at a table, sitting in a chair. Whenever I put my hands on the table or leaned on it, it rocked forward, one leg shorter than the rest making it impossible for the table to settle into an even plane.

It had been a long night. I'd fled the scene as quickly as I could and got home, locking all the doors, turning off all the lights. Joe texted me, "Dude!" Marvin texted an unhappy emoji. I texted Cici, my girlfriend. Five times. She didn't reply.

I tossed and turned for a bit and finally fell asleep. They came at 2:00 in the morning, pounding on my front door. I went without resistance. I'd seen what happens when a black man resists.

A door into the room was shut. Along one wall was a mirror that I knew was two-way. There were people back there watching, waiting to see if I'd sweat or somehow reveal guilt through my actions.

I didn't. I drummed my fingers on the table, whistled a happy tune, pretended to nap.

And a couple of hours after I was deposited in the room, the door opened. In stepped a police officer in uniform. He sat down across from me. Behind him came a detective in plain clothes. He closed the door and stood next to it, his back against the wall.

I waited to see which one would be the good cop, which one would be the bad. Turns out it didn't matter. They just gave it to me straight.

The detective spoke first. "You know why you're here?"

"Yeah, sure." I shrugged, picking up the drumming on the table again. "It's about what happened last night. At the game."

The detective spoke again, while the uniformed officer just stared at me. "Yes, the game. Somebody set off a fire alarm. 16,000 people panicked and tried to storm out of the arena all at once. Seventeen died. Over five hundred were hurt."

I didn't say anything. I waited. The officer filled the silence. "You know anything about it."

"Nope, not me." Listen. I knew. They knew I knew. I knew they knew I knew. And on and on. But I couldn't make it easy for them, could I? I had to put up a bit of a fight, even if it was pretty feeble.

The officer got up, walked around the table slowly, sat back down. "Well, that's interesting. We've got video from a security camera that shows you pulling the alarm. Same flannel shirt, faded jeans, mustache and bald patch at the back of your head." He put his hand on my drumming fingers, making me stop. "You want to see it?" He didn't take his hand off of mine.

"Well, it didn't end the way I expected, but at least nobody important died. Okay. I pulled the alarm. It was supposed to be a joke?"

"I'm thinking the families of those seventeen dead individuals might disagree. It's barely been twelve hours and they're already planning a memorial outside the arena for tonight. It's at 6:00. Maybe you should go?"

I shrugged again and looked at the officer, pulling my hand out from under his. It was kind of creepy to tell you the truth. His hand on mine, the sweat from his palm mingling with mine.

"Yeah, maybe." I decided to stall for time. Time for what, who knows? I'd just admitted to my role. "Can I get a cigarette?"

The detective pulled a pack out nowhere and gave me a cigarette. He had a lighter in his hand before I knew it and lit the end. I took a long drag and blew the smoke out.

"You said something interesting, Cole, about nobody important dying," The officer looked back at the detective who left his place by the door and took the last vacant seat at the table. He pulled out his phone and put it on the table. The uniform, Officer Smeltz by his nametag, continued, "Whose your favorite player on the Kings?"

"Hmmm. Hurley, probably."

"Yes, of course. Ellison Hurley IV. Everybody's favorite, right?"

Hurley was the sweet shooting guard drafted three years earlier. The smoothest release and biggest grin this side of Steph Curry. He'd put the Kings on his shoulders at the beginning of the season and ridden them to their first winning record in more than fifteen years. It was March, the playoffs were possible. Everybody loved him.

"Like I said. It was supposed to be a joke. My friends and I do stupid things. This was ..."

The detective interrupted me. "We knew Hurley is your favorite."

"Yes," I snapped. "He's everybody's."

"No, that's not why." He leaned over his phone and tapped the screen a couple of times, swiped up then left and then held it out to me. "Push play."

I did. The video was from a security camera in the Kings Corner, the store in the arena where they sold Kings branded gear. Everything from pencils to coffee cups to Christmas ornaments to shirts and jerseys of every type. The camera showed people running by outside the empty store for a few seconds and then I walked past the camera. Inside the store, which was empty since everybody was fleeing, I walked up to a rack and slipped a Hurley jersey off a hanger and put it on as I walked out of the store and joined the fleeing hordes.

"Okay," I tried for more nonchalance. "So what?"

"Hold on a sec," Officer Smeltz said. "There's more." He motioned to the detective, who picked up his phone and tapped and swiped a few more times.

This time the view was from a camera high up in the rafters, focused down on the corner of the arena where the Kings bench was. The detective told me, "We've got security cameras on everything. If you're at the game and pick your nose, we'll know about it. Push Play."

"Listen. I didn't realize this was going to happen. How could I know that a fire alarm pulled down in the loading area would set the whole damned mess off. I didn't realize there would be sprinklers. I didn't realize it would be that loud. I didn't realize ..." And that was the problem, I didn't realize that those sprinklers were more like water cannons and that the entire fire detection system was one completely integrated complex of alarms and signals and sprinklers and that all hell would break loose. I just didn't realize it.

"Push Play."

So, I did. For the first few seconds, it showed the Kings bench, the crowd behind. Everybody watching the action. Hurley was taking his early fourth quarter rest with a towel draped over his head. Suddenly, the shrill bleating sound of the arena's fire alarms pierced through and then the water cannons let loose and everybody was running. The view on the video shifted to another camera and it showed Hurley running towards the exit that took the players back to their locker rooms, there were fans and players in front of him and behind and they were all panicked.

I watched and saw what I didn't want to see. Just before he left the floor area, Hurley disappeared.

He went down. I didn't see him get up. The video shifted again. The fleeing crowd was gone, but on the floor, right where the parquet of the playing surface becomes the concrete leading into the bowels of the area, there was a body in a Kings uniform.

"Okay. Somebody important died." I looked up at Officer Smeltz as the video stopped. "I guess that's gonna be one hell of a memorial tonight."

Where This Came From: I'm an occasional participant in a Monday prompt writing group that meets locally. One week, the prompt was "nobody important." This is what came out. Don't ask me how or why.

* * * * *

She had brown hair that framed her face in waves and curls before dropping to her shoulders. Black-framed glasses that she didn't actually use to read the book she had open in her lap. Instead, they rested on her head, except when she slid them off and twirled them lazily with her right hand.

A backpack was at her feet. NYU on the front. When she first sat down and pulled the book out of her pack, she didn't bother closing it. I could see a textbook, a couple of notebooks. I imagined she was studying literature.

I imagined other things as well while I looked at her and the train sped along the tracks. When she was younger, did she like Pink Pony? What sports did she play, if she played any at all? She had the slender body of a runner. Maybe that was it. Or maybel soccer.

When she left home and went off to college, did she complain about not having a car even if she was headed to New York where the subway and walking were a way of life? Did she call home the first weekend in teears because she was scared and lonely?

"What are you reading?" I asked her quietly, almost afraid to ask. It was something I'd never done before.

The girl put her glasses on and looked at me. She held the book up so I could see the cover. *The Stranger* by Camus.

Maybe I was right. A literature student. Or just a reader. I was close to asking her if she had ever liked Pink Pony when the train got to my stop. It was probably better that way. I got up, she did too. I followed her out but lost her soon in the crowd that flowed out of the station and onto the city's streets.

Soon enough, though, I was on campus, looking for her. In the faces of the young women who went past me, hurring to class or laughing with friends. Not the girl on the train.

I was looking for my daughter. It had been ten years since she disappeared one night while walking back to her dorm room from a study session in the library. Her box of Pink Pony toys was still in her closet back home. Her books still lined the shelves.

I still wanted to know … what was she reading?

The Life Of A Shoe

At first, I was just parts. Eyelets here, laces there. A heel, a toe cap, quarters. A patterned sole. The label with a blue star. Converse. A high top.

In a factory on the outskirts of Bien Hoa, I became a shoe and then 14-year-old Cam Ho packaged me up in a box, wrapped in crinkly paper.

Size 9 ½. Matched with my mate. I was the right.

It got dark for a while. "Turn the damn lights on," I tried yelling. But my tongue didn't actually work like other tongues. Nobody heard me. It stayed dark too damn long. I began to wonder what was to become of me. I was meant for bigger things than a life stuffed in a box with a shoe I had never met until we were crammed together, even if I liked the crinkly paper.

And then ... one day the light came back on. I and my mate were on display in a Foot Locker in Eugene, lined up with other boxes of shoes. The lid off, the lights of the store shone brightly. I was ready for this. Damn it, some kid was going to look at us and say, "This pair. I want these."

In the land where Nike ruled, the section for Converse was pretty damn small. The orange Nike boxes with the god-damn stupid swooshes seemed like they were everywhere. Who would notice old school Converse high tops?

I held out hope though.

Days went by. Then weeks. Occasionally, I'd be lifted out of the box, put on a foot, laced up, walked around a bit. But always, I ended up back in the box, back on the shelf. I wanted to stop each kid who came in, "I'm the shoe for you. I've got a history. Take me and you'll see."

It happened finally. Johnny Mirengoff, with his mother, came into the store. He went straight for the Converses. "This is what Dad wore, right?"

"He did. But we can afford the Nikes. You don't need ..."

"Dad was an All-State point guard in his Converse. Let me at least try them on."

38

"Okay." I couldn't see Johnny's mother, but I heard something in her voice. A hitch maybe. A pause. All I really know is that I never saw Johnny's dad.

Because, yes, Johnny took me home with him that day. And yes, Johnny wore me and my mate on the hardwood, right where I was meant to be. I can't say he made All-State, but it was still a good year. Johnny guided the Churchill Lancers to their first Midwestern League Championship in years. Beyond that, the post-season tournament season was quick. The Lancers didn't make it out of the first round. Johnny made second team All Midwestern League.

And that was it, one year of running and squeaking on the hardwood of high school gyms throughout the Eugene area. I lived for those squeaks and for the pressure on my rubber sole when Johnny jumped and then landed. It was all good. I was where I was to be. Stuffed in a gym bag and then drawn back out, laced up, for another practice, another game. It really wasn't a year though.

After about six months and the end of the season, I made my way to the floor of Johnny's closet. Where I stayed, except for an occasional pick-up game.

It was okay. I had served my purpose. I had done what I was made for. Johnny was never going any further than high school. Too small, too slow for anything beyond that when it came to basketball. No matter what I did to try to make him faster, to jump higher, Johnny was damned to a basketball career that ended before it had barely begun.

It turned out that Johnny had another purpose though. A couple of years later, he enlisted. He went off to Afghanistan for one tour and then another. If I had any say in the matter, he wouldn't have done that. It sounded wrong, too dangerous, no real reward. But who was I? Just a shoe. With a purpose I never imagined.

I learned something though when Johnny left home. Every soldier has a good luck piece or two they walk with while they patrol the valley of death. Mike, who bunked next to Johnny on his first tour, had books. And he always took his Bible out with him on patrol. "It might just stop a bullet with my name on it," he frequently mumbled as he slid it into the front pocket of his shirt. Pablo had his mother's rosary beads.

Johnny? Johnny had his high tops. Me and my mate. I spent most of the time in his foot locker. But every once in a while, Johnny took us out.

With our laces tied together, he strung us around his neck. More rarely, he'd lace us up on his feet and play a rag tag game of basketball on the packed dirt of some base in the middle of the war zone.

One time, we went on a mission. "That shit ain't happening," Russell, the squad leader, said when he saw us draped around Johnny's neck.

"Aw, come on, Sarge. Pablo's got his beads. Chaplin's got that stupid hat – that's definitely not regulation." Johnny didn't remove us from around his neck. He just got in the Humvee and took his seat. Shotgun.

We were looking for a soldier who had walked off another base. Bergdahl was his name. We didn't find him.

But an IED found us. Buried in a pile of trash along the side of the road, it turned the Humvee upside down. Killed the driver. Ripped through Johnny, near took his right leg off. The doctors took care of the rest. Johnny would never have a right leg again. Never have a right foot. Never have a need for me again.

At least that's what I thought.

My mate? Somehow that blast tore our laces apart and when Johnny was medevac'd out of the place, he clutched me. Only me. I don't know what it was. A connection to his dad, who had died years earlier. To basketball. To Afghanistan and his brothers in arms he lived and died for. To something maybe even Johnny couldn't put words to.

When we got back to Eugene, where Johnny continued his recuperation, he kept me near him.

Johnny eventually got a prosthesis fitted. Connecting to his flesh just below his knee. A carbon blade for a foot. I wasn't sure what place I still had in his life. I damn sure wasn't going to be fitting on that blade.

For weeks and months, I was on top of his dresser. From that vantage point, I saw him sweat in the middle of the night, saw him cry when nobody else was around, saw him look at the bottle of pills and the gun he kept in his nightstand. I saw all of it.

It was Pablo who saved Johnny. He came to Eugene one day, barged into his room without knocking. Said, "Come on, dude. We're getting you out of here. Going on a f'in' adventure."

Just before Johnny followed Pablo out the door, he grabbed me and stuffed me in his backpack.

We drove to the coast that day. Walked along the edge of the ocean. Pablo didn't help Johnny at all. He made him do it all himself. Even when he fell, Pablo stood and waited for Johnny to get himself up. In Florence, they got ATVs and raced in the dunes. In the evening, Pablo and Johnny had a few beers and talked about things. About Afghanistan. About Johnny's pain. About Pablo's faith.

And finally, Pablo asked the $64,000 question, "What's with the shoe, Johnny?"

"What do you mean?"

"Come on, man. You've had that shoe with you forever. It's just a shoe." Pablo picked me up. "Getting kind of raggedy, too."

Well, hold on there just a hot second! Raggedy? RAGGEDY?!?! Johnny, you gotta defend me here. Tell him about the things we've done. The things we've seen. The luck I've brought you. Wait, back up a minute, maybe not that. But, come on. Raggedy? My ass. I'm a damn shoe. This is what I'm supposed to be.

"I don't know," Johnny replied. "Why do you keep those beads with you?"

"That's different. That's my faith."

"Maybe it isn't different." Johnny looked at Pablo and took a sip of his beer. "Maybe it's the same thing."

"Aw, come on. Are you seriously comparing 2,000 years of Catholicism with … what, a few pieces of leather and rubber?"

"Maybe I am. I don't know. It's just …" Johnny picked me up and turned me around in his hands. "My dad wore Converses and he's dead. Long gone before I ever got to know him. It's just … I need this like maybe you need those rosary beads? There are connections I make with this damn shoe …"

Damn shoe? No way, Johnny, I'm no damn shoe. You gotta do better than that!!

"I don't know." Johnny repeated, "I don't know."

"Hey, no worries," Pablo said. "You do what you gotta do, right?"

"Yeah. You do what you gotta do."

41

They lifted their glasses and clinked them together. "You do what you gotta do," they repeated in unison.

As the sun went down, we hit the road for the drive back to Eugene. The top was down on Pablo's Mustang. I was on the floorboards between Johnny's feet. Change that, switch that, back up a sec. Between his left foot and the blade that filled the space that once was his right foot.

I ached to be on his foot. I wanted to squeak with him on the hardwood again. I craved being something other than a good luck charm that had failed at his most basic of tasks. I …

Wait. What the heck is happening? I'm flying through the air. Johnny picked me up and looked at Pablo. "You're right about the shoe," he said, and then he flung me out of the car. I landed in the middle of the road, right between a couple of the yellow dashes that split the two lane road between Florence and Eugene.

Well, crap. What now? Johnny?

Where This Came From: My friend Mike, who lives in Eugene, Oregon, told me once about seeing a shoe in the middle of the road as he drove to the coast. Well, if that isn't a story prompt, what is?

* * * * *

The best day of my life

Followed by years of strife

For you, I battled and raged

Likely leaving you feeling caged

My desire for you to live your dreams

Drowned out by your petulant screams

I only wanted what I believed was the best

To help you reach and top the crest

No longer your hero

My opinion worth less than zero

It's the way it's supposed to be

You spread your wings to be free

Hardest thing though to be in the middle

Trying to solve the age old riddle

How does a father raise a son

When he wants to be of on his own, on the run.

The Last Dance

"Russia attacks Ukraine."

"Mr. President, Russia can't attack Ukraine. There is no Russia ..."

"Nyet! Russia attacks Ukraine." The President motioned at the board where it clearly said Ural and where he had amassed a sizable force. "There is no Ural. There is only Russia and Ukraine will soon become a part of it."

He rolled his three dice. 1, 2 and a 3.

Danilo, who had only two pieces left on the last country he had in the game, rolled two dice. 4 and 5. The President grumbled to himself and removed two pieces from Ural. 18 pieces remained.

"Again."

The President rolled. Nothing higher than a 4.

Danilo let his two dice scatter across the board. Two 5s. The President's grumble grew a little louder as he removed two more pieces.

"Let us switch dice." He took two of his and handed them to Danilo before picking up the two that remained on the board.

"Again."

And again, Danilo's roll topped the President's. Danilo began to sweat for he knew this was not how things were supposed to go when playing a game with the President. But still, the President's forces outnumbered his 14-2. Surely, his luck – good or bad depending on your perspective – would run out soon.

But it didn't. Four more rolls and the President's dominance had dwindled to 6-2. Danilo was on a roll.

"This is most unfortunate," the President said. "I must fortify Russia." He swept ten more pieces from a neighboring country and ended his turn. Danilo could do nothing. No pieces from neighboring countries would come to the aid of Ukraine. He smiled at the President, "I pass."

Before he took his turn, the President picked up all five dice and shook them in his hand. "I take these," he said as he picked out three, "and you get these." He dropped two on the board.

The President rolled. Danilo rolled. And once again, two of the President's pieces were removed from Ural. "Nyet!" the President exclaimed. "Russia must win."

"Again!"

A few turns later, with the same results in hand, the President looked at Danilo across the board. He turned then to one of his aides and whispered in his ear.

"Again!" As the President rolled his dice, the aide rose and left the room, and when Danilo rolled and again defeated the President, the aide returned with two security officers. They walked directly to Danilo and one of them said, "Please. Come with us."

"I ... it's just a game," Danilo pleaded.

"There is no such thing as a game," the President stated. "Russia always wins." He looked at the officers and nodded his head. Each took one of Danilo's arms and picked him up from his chair and walked him out of the room.

"Now," the President looked around the room. "You," he said to the aide and motioned to the empty chair.

"Y-y-yes," the aide said, reluctantly settling in the chair and picking up the two dice.

"Again!"

And the results were the same. As turn by turn rolled by, the President kept losing. At one point, he was able to eliminate one of the remaining pieces on Ukraine, but still that one piece and its corresponding die were steadfast in their defense against the President's forces.

When the President had finally moved all of his available forces to Ural and those had been wiped out, but for one piece, the final move occurred.

"AGAIN!" the President shouted, his face red, sweat pouring down his forehead, his anger at a fever pitch. "AGAIN!" he repeated as he rolled the die. Five pips showed up on top.

The aide looked at the single die in his hand, looked at his boss, and prayed in his mind for something less. Anything less than a 5. He had a two-thirds chance of his prayer coming true. He knew that luck would not be with him if he rolled a 6.

"Roll!" the President yelled at him, taking a handkerchief from his pocket and wiping the sweat from his brow.

The aide let the die fall from his hand and swore under his breath. Six pips showed. He looked at his boss as the President lifted his eyes from the board and made eye contact. Locked on his aide's eyes, the President slammed his hands down on the table. "Nyet! Russia never loses! I never lose!!" He rose and pointed his finger at his aide. "You! Out!"

The door opened and more security officers entered the room. The aide cowered in his seat, knowing what would come next. Either a quick death or a long train ride to Siberia. He prayed for his wife and children and that he might see them again. But the security officers bypassed the aide and went to the President's chair.

"Come with us," said the officer with the biggest epaulets on his shoulders.

"What?! Me?" the President yelled again. "It is him. He is a traitor and has defeated the Motherland!"

The officer stepped forward as another stepped to the other side of the President. They put their hands under the President's elbows. "Come with us," the one officer said again.

"But I am the President!" He pounded the table again and began to cry and scream in unrecognizable gibberish that poured out of his mouth.

"Yes … you were. But you lost the Motherland in a foolish onslaught that served no purpose." They roughly stood him up and with the officers forming a cordon around him, walked the President out of the room.

Where This Came From: I wanted to write something about the lunacy of the Russian invasion of Ukraine. This is it. This story is the first of several that are derived from real life events. *An Obituary* and *Aleppo* are a couple of others that are included in this collection. This piece was published at *The Disappointed Housewife*.

To Osaka blows
Wind waving the pampas grass
Good-bye love, life fades

To Osaka blows
Swirling, shivering wind, snow
Drying with summer

Wing waving the pampas grass
Two lovers lay, sun shines down
Moments, hours, days

Good-bye love, life fades
Cold returns, an end, no more
To Osaka blows

Memories of Foom

His name was Foom Xiong. I knew he came from the lowlands of Laos and that his mother's name was True. He would speak of her in the quiet nights when we slept in the dark without light or noise above a whisper. I'll never forget the gleaming white of his eyes the moonlight created as he described his mother. A woman who bore three children. Foom the youngest of the bunch. His father wandered off to the endless wars of Southeast Asia and never returned.

When Foom was old enough, so did he. He was ferocious, fighting without fear, laughing in the face of death.

I didn't know his age though, but I knew he was young. Likely too young to be the fierce fighter he was, too young to be out in the jungles instead of at home helping his mother. Maybe though it was in the jungles where he learned what he needed. Found his purpose. I don't know. I just know I came to depend on him. His fighting skills, his sense of humor, and the stories he told in his broken English.

Foom was with us as the Vietnam War wound down. He begged, "Please ... with you." Every day we moved closer to Hue where our troop was being evacuated from. He said it as a statement, a fact that he would be able to leave the only land he had known. His eyes and how they pleaded betrayed his lack of confidence.

"I'll see when we get there," was the best I could offer. I doubted little Foom, no matter how fiercely he had fought for us, would be high on the priority list.

In Hue, at the airbase gate, American soldiers were allowed through while the poor soldiers who had fought with us were kept from entering by MPs. Sometimes the MPs had to fire their guns into the air. It didn't faze Foom though. As I walked towards the entrance, he stayed with me as close as he could. Maybe he hoped he would melt into my shadow and be invisible to the guards manning the gate.

It didn't work. The MPs moved to separate Foom and me. "Stop!" they shouted as two MPs jumped between us with their guns brandished.

"Please," Foom begged, reaching for me. "Mr. Joe ... America ... I want America."

The soldiers stood firmly between us while I tried to convince them Foom was okay. They just shook their heads, kept their guns at the ready, and said, "No natives allowed."

They began to push Foom back when he reached his hand out to me. In his hand was a bunch of pictures and papers rolled up and wrapped in a piece of twine. "Please, Mr. Joe, take."

I reached for them, while he continued. "Pictures GIs take of me, my village. Come find me again," he wailed as the MPs pushed him far enough away that I lost hope of changing the tide. I stood there and watched him swallowed up by the massed locals who were trying to find a way on to the base and a plane that would take them away. I kept my eyes on him as long as I could. His eyes. His mouth. He smiled at one point. I heard him yell one last time, "Mr. Joe," before he was gone.

I returned home. I kept his pictures and papers in a box in my closet. No matter where I lived, the box was always there. Occasionally, I'd thumb through the contents, see Foom's picture and remember his stories and his laugh. When I did, I would ask the picture, "Where did you end up, Foom? Are you still back at home in the lowlands or did you make it here to America?"

Years later, I had raised my own two kids, one of whom joined the military and was lost during the battle for Fallujah. He came back in pieces and was buried in the National Cemetery in Dixon. I visited him every now and then, telling him of my memories of Foom and of the things that were going on in my life. The divorce, the loneliness, the memories.

One day, I went for a walk through a cemetery down the street from my home. It was an old cemetery with historic sections and newer sections as well. As I stumbled along reading gravestones and walking through shade and sunlight, I found a grave marker that stopped me.

True Xiong

July 4, 1928 – September 25, 2010

I looked at those dates and the reference to children and grandchildren left behind below the dates. My mind whirred, trying to do the math. It certainly seemed possible. A plastic butterfly attached to a plastic bouquet of flowers on the grave reminded me that Foom told me how much his mom loved butterflies.

Foom's mother was buried beneath the ground I stood on, which could only mean one thing. He had made it to America, for his mother surely would not have come without her children. He had been here in my town. Maybe even living in my neighborhood. For years, I had been so close to him.

I couldn't help myself, I twirled around thinking he might be there, watching me and making his own mental calculations. Spanning forty years of separation, with only faded pictures and dimmer memories, would we have recognized each other? Had I seen him at some point, not knowing it was Foom I saw?

The pleasure and pain of this knowledge burned a hole in me that day. The next, I gathered the papers and pictures Foom had handed me across the line in the base at Hue. I put them in an envelope, wrapped it in tape so it would be somewhat water proof and went back to the cemetery. I left the package on the grave with a note from me included. It said simply, "Mr. Joe wants to see you." And included my phone number.

I went back home and waited.

Where This Came From: When I got my digital SLR camera, one of the first things I did was go to a nearby cemetery, a very historic place, to take pictures. One of the pictures I took was of a grave marker for True Xiong, which I recognized to likely be somebody from Laos. Around the marker was an empty bottle of wine and a dried flower arrangement. I thought there was a story to be told from that.

The Rosewood

They came from all over and lived for a time at 214 Olive Street. Some lived there for decades. Others only for a few years. They all called it home. At least for a time. The complex, built in the 1950s, was small by modern standards. Just three buildings, two floors each, one unit on top and one on bottom. Arranged in an odd triangle that created an even odder courtyard in the middle. All angles and straight lines, nooks and crannies, caused by the three buildings. Every unit, the same floor plan. A bedroom, a living area, kitchen, and bathroom.

Out in front, there were letters attached to a wall that identified the place as Rosewood Apartments. The tenants referred to it as 'The Rosewood.' In the evenings, whoever was around gathered in the courtyard and shared in the dying light of each day.

From #1 came Janie, who did not have a gun. Instead, she had a tattoo from her days in the Navy. Yes, it's not just old guys from the 1940s with an anchor on their bicep to show their allegiance. Janie, who was in the first group of women allowed to serve on warships in 1994, got the tattoo. It was a rite of passage. A commitment to her service. A need to show she was just as tough as the guys on the ship. The U.S.S. Roosevelt. Named after the first President Roosevelt, not the second.

It hurt. Damn, it hurt. But she didn't cry. She gritted her teeth and got through it. Only later, when Janie was in her bunk and it was dark did she let tears course down her cheeks as she quietly relived the pain of the needle.

Janie served ten years before getting out. She had done what she set out to do – she was as tough as the men and she had the damn anchor tattoo to show for it. When she got out, Janie returned home. Not to her parents' home, where she had spent her childhood, but to the hometown. Sacramento. Where she moved into The Rosewood, scraping together rent money out of her small military pension and the tips she earned working at the pizza place down the street.

It was the life she lived and she was okay with it. Never married. No kids. A few friends here and there. A simple life with little expectation and even less fear. In the evenings, when the neighbors gathered in the courtyard, Janie brought her backgammon board.

In #2, above Janie's was Sheldon, who everybody called Shel. The newest arrival at The Rosewood, Shel moved in a year before the owners provided notice that of the pending demolition. He wanted to fight it, get the rest together and take the owners to court. Show up at city council meetings. Talk to the local newspaper. Do something. Anything to make it stop.

Shel worked at a health club, handing out towels and wiping down equipment. He took yoga classes and ran on the treadmill, only occasionally lifting weights. On his days off, Shel went for runs along the river and met with friends for a beer afterwards.

Those who gathered in the courtyard seemed resigned to their fate. No matter how much he pushed them, pleaded and begged, nothing changed. "We're only a few people. Who's gonna care about us," Janie said when she had finally heard enough. "Nobody. That's who."

"But what about Rebecca?" Shel asked.

Rebecca, who lived in #3. Rebecca, sweet, wonderful Rebecca. She had moved into The Rosewood a couple of years before Shel. A year later, her parents died in a freak accident. Her old man's life insurance policy paid off to the tune of $250,000. But she didn't move. She stayed right where she was.

Rebecca had a very healthy case of agoraphobia. The money went into the bank. She stayed in her apartment. DoorDash, Instacart, and countless other delivery services were her lifelines to the outside world.

There were a few months, after she moved into The Rosewood, when Rebecca was just like everybody else. Working, hanging out in the courtyard, doing the downtown social scene. Until one day, she just stopped. If asked, and she was never actually asked by any of her neighbors, she would have told them.

It was because of the homeless man who occasionally slept in the complex's entryway. He muttered things to her when she walked by him. Late in the evenings, when it was dark and all she could really see of him were the whites of his eyes in the pool of darkness that was the entryway. Whispering to her about how she looked and how she smelled. The words wheedled their way into her brain until she ... just ... couldn't do it anymore.

Rebecca quit her job and stayed holed up in her apartment, never, ever leaving. The insurance payoff was a big deal for her.

Janie thought about Shel's question and she almost answered one way, before changing her mind. "She'll just have to figure it out."

What Janie really wanted to do was reveal that she, as well as everybody else at The Rosewood, knew of Shel's little secret. He had a girlfriend in the 'burbs. He grumbled and moaned about the commute to see her, enough that somebody would regularly ask him, "Why don't you two find a place together?"

Shel would hem and haw and spit out something like, "That's just not a good idea right now."

"Why not?"

"Just ... because."

But they all knew the real reason. Shel and Rebecca had a thing. Her agoraphobia didn't stop him from visiting her every now and then.

It was Steffani in #4 who figured it out. Steffani was a career student. Bachelor's degrees in sociology and psychology. Years spent on her Master's degree and accompanying thesis while she took more classes, most of which did nothing other than fill her days and weeks.

One night, Steffani heard noises from beneath her, waking her from a dead sleep. Noises like ... somebody was having sex! What the hell was going on, she wondered. Her curiosity kept her awake and then when she heard Rebecca's door open, it drew her to her curtain as she watched Shel return to his apartment. "Good for her," she thought. "She may not leave her apartment, but she apparently has invited Shel in."

Steffani, whose car had the most sensitive alarm in the history of car alarms. In the scramble for parking spots on the street outside of The Rosewood, she occasionally hit the lottery and found a spot right outside. When she did, the other tenants would curse their own rotten luck. Chances were, her alarm would go off several times those nights. Waking her neighbors, but oddly, never her. The noises of Rebecca and Shel's activities, which continued beyond just that one night, somehow did. But all the beeping and sirens and noises emitted by her alarm rarely did.

54

Those who lost sleep tried to talk to her about it. Janie asked her, "Why can't you disconnect it?"

"Are you kidding me? It stops thieves!" Steffani replied.

"How? You apparently never hear it."

"So."

Shel told her to "turn the damn thing off" more than a few times.

The end result was that Steffani rarely came to the courtyard gatherings. She felt a shunning and was powerless to prevent it.

Until, of course, she disclosed her secret. One night when Shel was with his girlfriend and the rest of the crowd was gathered, she slipped into the mix and told Tom, who lived in Unit #5, what she had seen. And heard.

Well, you know how these things go. Soon, everybody was talking about Shel and Rebecca, except, of course, for Shel and Rebecca.

Tom, now, he had a sympathetic ear for Steffani. The tenants bitched and moaned about him too. But how could he help it. He played the trombone for the Sacramento Symphony and he had to practice a lot in #5.

Once again it was Janie, it always seemed to be Janie from Tom's perspective, who complained. "Can't you practice somewhere else? Aren't there places for you to do that?" she whined to him one day.

"Sure there are, but they cost money," Tom replied. "Do you know how little I get paid playing for the symphony. I'm barely getting by as it is. Paying for a place to practice would break the bank. You know?"

"Jeez," she said. "It's just kind of difficult for me, for the rest of us, when you're practicing constantly."

"That's too bad." Tom shrugged. "It would be nice if you appreciated my talent instead of finding it offensive."

They didn't talk much after that. Keeping their distance in the courtyard gatherings and grumbling 'hello' when they crossed paths. It was a shame because, at one point, Tom was the only one who could beat Janie at backgammon.

Five of the six units were occupied by single people. #6 was occupied by the only family. Hasib and Aaela, and their little boy, Hamid. Refugees from Afghanistan, they were whisked into the only empty unit one night. For weeks, they barely left, never coming to the courtyard gatherings. At times, the curtains in their front room, which looked out over the courtyard would part, fingers visible on the curtain, but not much else.

Members of a nearby church brought them food every few days and eventually Hasib began to leave early in the morning to drive a taxi around the city's streets. And gradually, they joined the courtyard talks. First, Hasib, who revealed he had worked as a translator for the U.S. during the war. That they had escaped with the clothes on their backs and not much else.

Soon Aaela came out with her husband, bringing lavash and lamb to share, or bolani with dipping sauces. She always smiled quietly and sat with her husband, letting him do the talking. Their little boy, Hamid, was quiet as well, but eventually he opened up and, as small boys do, brought laughter and play to the courtyard crowd when he was there.

They'd lived there for three years, eschewing the places where refugees tended to live together, preferring the home they made among these Americans. Hamid soon went off to school during the day and practiced his English with Shel and Janie, Steffani and Tom.

While once they gathered quietly over the years to spend their days and nights at The Rosewood, when the news came that the place was set to be demolished, the evening conversations took on a different tone. They were given three months' notice. Three months and $2,000 to find a solution. Conversations that all too frequently turned into arguments as those who wanted to do something ran head long into the apathy of those who had given up.

Hasib pleaded with his neighbors, joining Shel, "We must do something. You have taken us in. You are our family. Our boy," he brought Hamid onto his lap and tousled his hair, "speaks more of each of you than anybody else in his life."

Shel, as previously noted, concurred. Strongly. "H is right. Dammit!" He stood up. "There has to be a way to fight this."

"How," more than one of the others asked when push came to shove. "How," they repeated.

It was a question nobody had a real answer to. The media. Their council member. Protests in the streets. Chaining themselves to an immovable object? Everything was thrown out and shot down for not being enough because, in truth, they were not enough. Who would care about a handful of residents of an old apartment complex when developers were planning on replacing it with a six-story building with condos for the rich and influential. How could they compete with that?

In the end it was Rebecca who brought them a bit of time. With a week to go, none of them had moved. An inertia had befallen all of them. A disbelief that they would actually have to leave. A belief instead that something would change. That something was Rebecca when she called out from her window while they argued once again. "I'm not leaving," she yelled to them. "They'll have to cart my dead body out to get me out of here."

Her declaration united the others to action. "Save Rebecca!" they shouted. "Save The Rosewood!" they roared. In the days ahead, all but Rebecca picketed in front of City Hall. A local news station ran a story on their efforts.

On the second Monday of May, the demolition crew showed up anyway. None of the tenants had moved. If Rebecca wasn't leaving, neither were they. The foreman scratched his head when he saw that they were all still there and called his boss who called the developer.

By noon, the developer was on-site arguing with the tenants, who remained in their places.

In the months that followed, a court order was obtained by the developer. A team from the Sheriff's Department showed up to enforce the court order. And still the tenants didn't move. They stayed for months, after a contempt order was issued. After the cops showed up again. They stayed.

Until, eventually, they tired of the effort. First, Janie left, moving a few blocks over. Then, Hasib and his family departed for one of those complexes in the suburbs filled with other refugees from Afghanistan. Then it was Tom, who took his trombone, and Steffani, who drove her car off to another town and another life. And finally, all that was left were Shel and Rebecca.

In the dead of night, they left together. Finding an apartment they could share. The girlfriend was no more. It was just Shel and Rebecca, who still wouldn't leave once they got settled.

Where This Came From: Reedsy is an on-line resource for writers. They run a weekly prompt contest with five different prompts each week. This is a response to the following prompt: write a story about an apartment building that is about to be demolished.

An Obituary

His name was Sebastian Cole.

His friends called him Bas 'cause that's what his brother Wilson called him. The three syllables were too much for the little guy. Bas was all he could handle. It stuck.

Others called him Sebastard 'cause that's what kids do.

His Mama called him Baby, but she called all her kids that. It was nothing special. The neighborhood kids who filtered in and out. The foster kids who showed up for a month or a year. They were all Baby. 'Cause everybody was her baby, her love tending them and protecting them.

His Papa called him nothing. He wasn't there.

He played little league for a year or two. Basketball in the 8th grade. Nothing after that. His Mama told him schooling was what mattered.

It started to unravel for Bas just before he graduated. Something happened. A girl maybe. A poor score. It coulda been. But, he had a funk. Missed school for a couple of weeks, barely got back in time for the ceremony.

It aint nothin' his Mama told him. You'll be just fine. College'll be in a few months. You'll get right with yourself.

Sure Mama, he replied. And he thought that. Really thought that. He signed up for classes at the community college. Got a job at McDs.

Bas lost the job a few months later when he was found muttering to himself. Back by the sink. Staring at the wall. When his manager asked him what was up, he spun around and spat at him. Bas told him he wasn't no monkey.

Truth is, after a couple of weeks, he stopped going to class. It wasn't for him.

He was arrested for the first time when he was nineteen. He jaywalked and talked back to the officer who wrote him up. White boys jaywalked there all the time he said, never got no citations.

The officer said, Boy, you gotta a problem? Bas didn't back down. He spent the night in a jail cell.

The voices started shortly after that. Telling him to do this. Do that. Some days he never got out of bed. Some weeks he never left the house.

His Mama kept asking, Baby, you okay? He had nothing for her. Just leave me alone, he'd say.

She did until she couldn't anymore.

You need to get on outta here, Sebastian Cole, she yelled one day.

So he got on outta there.

Found a spot under an overpass. Found a ragged blanket. Got a shopping cart from the market. Scrounged for things. This and that.

Bas spent his days going from soup kitchen to soup kitchen.

Come. Stay for a bit. We'll have a room for you tonight, they'd say to him.

Bas would smile sometimes and say, no thank you. Other times, he might growl, maybe even raising a fist before stomping away, cart in tow.

He got arrested again. Kicked out of a spot for illegal camping, he raged at the officer, pushed him back. Cuffs slapped on, he showed up inn county jail with some bruises that weren't there moments before.

A few years went by. The voices got louder. The streets harder. Sometimes he thought he saw his Mama on the street. Bas would approach her, asking for help. She'd turn away saying, I can't help you. I'm sorry. Sometimes, she'd give him a dollar or two.

One day, Bas found a gun behind a trash bin. He released the clip. Saw there were two bullets.

The gun went buried in the middle of his cart. Beneath the old blanket and the bag of recycling.

Sebastian Cole found one of his favorite spots that night. Where a vent spread warm air and he could curl up against it and stay warm. In the middle of the night the voices rose to a crescendo and woke him. Get the gun, they wailed in his head. Get the gun.

He did. Holding it in his hand. Looking at the glimmer of the street lights reflecting off its cold, black steel.

Sebastian Cole's final moments were spent sitting on a concrete ledge, under pine trees that had stood guard over the old state building for almost one hundred years. His Mama wasn't there to protect her Baby. The voices told him he had no choice. He held the gun to his mouth.

Where This Came From: I arrived at work one morning to find police tape around a portion of the west side of the building. There was a body there. I decided the body needed a story.

Aleppo

"Papa. I'm scared." Sami whispered.

"Ssshhh," his Papa whispered back. "There is no reason to be scared. We will be going soon. Where we will be safe."

They whispered in the dark. In the cold. Their breath creating misty clouds.

Once upon a time Papa was a baker. He owned a little shop on Nile Street, just down from the Alforat traffic circle. For years, Papa's kollaj and zarda fed the masses. Lines at Rifat's were not uncommon. They came for his halva and stayed for his awameh. They took home Rifat's baloza. And in the darkness of an Aleppo night, they shared it with their families, their friends, their neighbors.

Whether Alawi or Sunni or Shia. Druze or Christian. Sect didn't matter. Religion was what one did in one's home. In one's mosque or church. This was Aleppo after all.

They came for his pastries and his treats.

Until they didn't.

* * * * *

Refugees from Syria over 10k plus more coming. Lots young males, poorly vetted. @RealDonaldTrump

* * * * *

At first Rifat thought that maybe it was just one of those swings. Sometimes things slowed. Sometimes things picked up. In moments, he wondered if he might make it. In others, he thought he might need to hire help. That he surely needed to keep the lines moving faster. Those other times -- when the line formed early in the morning with workers, replaced

62

later by government clerks, and then filled in by the women of the neighborhood who wanted a treat for the table-- were more than they weren't. Rifat was successful. He dreamed of an education for his little Sami. Maybe of a little house in the wooded hills of his childhood, where he could return in his final days.

Then there was a bomb. An explosion. Just down the street. Past Alforat, but close enough that he felt the shock. The windows of his little bakery shook. Flour dust rose and then settled again. And for a moment Rifat worried about his family. About his wife, Rima, and the little one, Haya. And Sami, his son. His legacy. The little boy who laughed in the light and trembled in the dark. Rifat could tell the explosion was not near his home, but still. An explosion in Aleppo. The rebels. The fight. He supported it. He wanted it. An end to Assad and his treachery. His brutality.

But he was a simple baker who wanted nothing more than to make a living, love his family, and see the next day. And dream his dreams.

He ran to the door. To the street. To Alforat. He saw clouds of dust thrown into the cloudless sky. Heard the wailing sirens ululating and echoing down the cement corridors. He ran no further. He had seen enough.

Rifat closed his bakery for the day. He returned home and held Rima and told her it was temporary. That Assad would soon be gone and life would be better. He quieted Sami and Haya. He heard the stories later of the dozens killed. One day he walked past the rubble. Little did he know that day that the rubble would remain for years to come.

In the morning, before the sun rose, he returned to the bakery. He kneaded the dough. Mixed the spices. Opened his doors. And the line wasn't there. Instead, somebody on a motorcycle sped by and a man on the back threw a brick through his window.

* * * * *

If I had a bowl of Skittles and I told you just three would kill you. Would you take a handful? That's our Syrian refugee problem. #MakeAmericaGreatAgain

* * * * *

Rifat closed early. Boarded the window and prayed that it would be all. He had seen the stories of Tunis and of Tahrir. He knew of the treachery of his own government in years and decades past. Of chemical weapons and of villages leveled. He wanted a change, but his bakery was his everything. He prayed that the revolution would come but that its damage would pass him by. Stay in Damascus. Or in the hills and villages. Aleppo was a cosmopolitan city of tolerant people. A boarded window was nothing, he knew. He hoped. He prayed.

Soon though Rifat's business changed. As the fighting grew closer, as lines were drawn, Rifat did what he could. Instead of the pastries and treats he had been known for, he began to make pita by the basket and handed it to those who stumbled by his shop. Far too many of them were children, coated in dust, shell-shocked expressions on their faces.

The bombs fell more frequently. The sirens wailed all too often. Chlorine gas that left so many choking and gasping. Families wiped out. Children orphaned. Those that remained knew nothing other than hunger and fear and despair. The least he could do was turn his dwindling supplies and what he could gather from the bakery's back door in the dark hours of the morning into bread to feed the hungry.

* * * * *

Just tried watching Saturday Night Live - unwatchable! Totally biased, not funny and the Baldwin impersonation just can't get any worse. Sad @RealDonaldTrump

* * * * *

Haya was the first. The dark days of a cold winter, while the war raged in other places but Aleppo lay in mutual states of siege. Rebels on one side of the line, the government on the other. Nothing got in. Nobody got out. More days when he had nothing to bake with than those when he could.

When his little girl began coughing and burning hot, Rifat searched for medicine. He begged at the makeshift clinics, where the wind whistled through tarps that covered the holes in the walls, and nobody was warm. Rifat offered bribes to doctors who looked at him out of haggard faces, their eyes sad. All he got was a shake of the head and little Haya coughed some more. Wheezing and rattling, the skin around her rib cage sucking in when she tried to take a breath. Her eyes sinking into dark circles.

Rima pleaded with Rifat, "You must do something." He could only beg some more. His baking could not heal Haya.

And so she died one cold, dark night, bundled between Rifat and Rima. Her breathing labored, her eyes rolled back into her head. Sami slept nearby. In the morning they bundled her up. Sami sobbing. Rima in a quiet daze. Rifat stone-faced. They took her to the hospital where they said she was dead. There was nothing they could do for her. "But we will take her body for you."

Haya's body was taken to the basement where it was left with the others. Rima sat in a corner of their home where she could look out the window. It seemed she never blinked. It seemed she didn't see a thing. Rifat didn't know how to reach her. He could only walk through the room, slowing as he went, thinking of something to say. But no words came. He moved through to the kitchen.

* * * * *

Has anyone looked at the really poor numbers of VanityFair Magazine. Way down, big trouble, dead! Graydon Carter, no talent, will be out! #RealDonaldTrump

* * * * *

Rifat returned to his bakery, making pita when he could. When he had the ingredients for it. When he didn't, he sat at his counter and counted the hours. The minutes. The seconds. What was once a busy street now stood mostly empty. People rushed from corner to corner, huddling in doorways, looking to the sky. Sure, the men gathered in his bakery and sometimes he closed his door and walked down to Akram's grocery where the men huddled amidst the empty shelves and the coolers that no longer had power to keep their empty spaces cold.

They talked of Assad and the rebels. Akram's son had joined the Islamic State and was in Raqqa. Majd's was with the Nusra Front. His brother-in-law was on the other side of the line, fighting for Assad. Fathi's son was dead. As was Tarek's. And Marwan's. Ali's.

They talked of escaping, but they heard the stories of those who had tried. Camps where refugees gathered and stayed hungry and cold, if they were able to survive the gauntlet of Hezbollah fighters, government troops, of bombs and land mines. Besides, Aleppo was home.

They remained and grew hungrier and sicker and more and more dead every day. Rifat could do nothing more than trudge from his home to his bakery and back. To speak tonelessly with the men who gathered. Stare while Sami played. Look at Rima from a distance and wonder if she would ever smile again. Would he?

The streets grew more desolate. The buildings, one after another, were turned into rubble. First it was buildings, then it was blocks. Neighborhoods laid in ruins. Their home was safe. Or so it seemed.

When the helicopters came and the barrel bombs were pushed out their doorways, Sami was with Rifat at the bakery, playing with a ball of dough. Flour on his nose and in his hair. For a moment, a strange noise rose from Rifat's belly. He laughed. And then he heard the booms and the ground shook and the noises came from the wrong direction. He picked his little boy up and he ran, holding his breath. Around the corner, down the street.

All he found was an arm, with the tattered sleeve of the thawb he had seen her wearing when he left the house that morning.

* * * *

Reports by CNN that I will be working on The Apprentice during my Presidency, even part time, are ridiculous & untrue - FAKE NEWS!

* * * *

66

A year passed. Truces came. Truces went. When the Russians arrived, it only got worse. Promises made. Promises broken. The bombs grew bigger, the destruction greater. They got hungrier and sicker and colder and more and more dead. The rebels and civilians who occupied their little corner of Aleppo were broken. Only they didn't know it yet.

Sami had shrunk. Instead of growing as little boys are supposed to, his growth had stopped. He rarely played anymore. He mostly sat on his Rifat's lap, where they could keep each other warm. To Rifat, his little boy felt as light as a bag of twigs. He feared he would lose Sami too.

The men began to talk of a new agreement. The rebels would be allowed to leave. Assad would retake their corner of Aleppo. Civilians could decide to stay or to go.

Rifat had no delusions about what would happen to the civilians who stayed. After years of bombings and snipers and thousands of civilians dying in the streets of Aleppo, he had no doubt what the Assad government thought of the civilians. He would never feel safe under Assad's thumb.

He agreed to leave Aleppo. To re-settle somewhere else. For Sami. For himself. He needed to dream again.

In the quiet, Rifat hushed Sami. He tried not to shiver. But the morning was cold as the sun rose to chase the dark away. There were buses lined up to take them and others out of Aleppo. To one of the camps the men used to talk about.

Soon he was in a line at one of the buses. And then they were in the bus and they were leaving Aleppo. It was only thirty minutes before the bombs began to fall. All along the row of buses, snaking through the hills to a camp. Rifat saw flames shooting out of other buses and then the bus they were in was struck and the flames engulfed him. He didn't know whether it was Hezbollah or the Syrian Army or the Russians. But for a second or two, he knew he would never be cold again. That he would never be afraid again.

Where This Came From: At the height of the Syrian Civil War, I wanted to write a story about somebody trying to survive there, while creating a juxtaposition to the madness that infects American politics.

* * * * *

A mistake
Of epic proportions
A shame
A tragedy
Of human making
A blotch
An infection
No antibiotic can cure
A boil
A wound
That cuts deep, too deep
A scab
A curse
On our name
A blister
A rejection
Of our history and traditions
A degradation
A failure
Of moral leadership

As of June 2012, when I wrote this, 169 men remained at Guantanamo Bay – with Abu Ghraib, enhanced interrogation techniques, and rendition – one of the pillars of this country's shame following the attacks on 9/11. And, it continues. In Spring 2022, 37 detainees remain there.

Beelzebub & Lucifer

I woke up feeling that something wasn't quite right. Maybe it was because Beelzebub wasn't at the foot of the bed.

No, the devil doesn't sleep in my bed with me. Well, as long as you don't count Audra. She was the devil and she slept in my bed for a couple of years. Until I was able to get rid of her. No. Beelzebub was my dog. An English bulldog, with all of the muttering and snuffling and drooling that comes along with the breed.

But when I sat up, Beelzebub was on the floor, laying in his bed. He did that some times. So, that wasn't it.

I called him and he lifted his head and looked at me with those eyes. The ones that first pulled me to him at the pound. They were sad, always sad, but there was a gleam in them, too. A sparkle that told me the sadness was just an affect - a look he couldn't help. It wasn't how he felt. He slowly stood up, stretching as he did so, and trundled over to the side of the bed. I dangled my hand down and scratched the wrinkled fur that formed around his neck. He snuffled a bit to reward my efforts.

But things still didn't feel right. I sniffed at the air. All I got was the stench of sweat-soaked sheets. I rose and went to the window and looked out. The world looked as it usually did. A few cars made their way down the street. The doorman at the apartment across the street. Baxter, stood where he always stood. White gloves looking snappy. His epaulets at attention. When old lady Smithers waltzed up with her little foo-foo dog, he bent slightly at the waist and then opened the door for her. Once she was safely inside and the door swung shut behind her, the doorman smirked and twirled his finger around his ear. Yeah, everything was okay out there. All per usual.

I stood and went to the bathroom. As I did my business, I cast my mind through the rest of the apartment. And that's when it hit me. The bird

69

was quiet. Usually, with the first light of day, the damn macaw -- left behind by Audra -- was talking smack to the sun. Lucifer's morning conversation was what usually woke me up. I checked the clock on my nightstand on my way out of the bedroom. Damn. I'd overslept by an hour. Good thing I was still working from home. The commute wasn't going to be a problem, and I could still log on and "work" by 8:00.

In the family room, I went to Lucifer's cage. She was perched there, looking at me. "Lucifer, what's up?" He lifted his wings and squawked at me. "Everything okay?"

"Bite me!" she said.

Yes. I taught her that.

"Suck off."

Audra taught her that.

So, Lucifer was fine. It wasn't that. Beelzebub padded up behind me and looked up. There was something that still didn't feel right. I turned around and looked around the apartment and that's when I smelled it. A scent I recognized. One that I hadn't experienced in the two years since Audra had left. It smelled like her perfume. Eternity. I had learned to hate that smell. Sensing it now made me gag. Just a bit.

"Beelzebub, where is that coming from?"

"Over here."

"What did you say?" I looked down at the dog, then over at the bird. If a bird could shrug, Lucifer did just that.

"Over here," the voice said again. With my eyes on Lucifer, I can attest that it wasn't the damn bird. And then I realized that I recognized the voice, just as I had recognized the scent.

70

I walked around the sofa so I could see the front of it. There she was. Audra, laying there with not a stitch of clothing. "How ... how did you get in?"

"You never asked for your spare key back." She winked. "Surprise."

Yes. Indeed. Surprise. Something was most definitely not quite right. I'm not ashamed to admit that I screamed then and raced for my bedroom. Slamming the door. Locking it. And then praying to a god I didn't believe in.

My prayers weren't answered. Audra didn't walk out of the apartment, leaving me to my content solitude. No, of course not. She was the devil, remember.

Shortly after I closed the door and turned the lock, there was a light knocking at the door. I stopped my mumbled prayers, looked for a place to hide, and began to pray again. Quietly, so the she-devil wouldn't hear me. "Please, please, oh please, make her go away. I will give myself up to you, if you can do that."

God clearly wasn't listening. Or didn't care.

"Honey," came Audra's voice from the other side of the door. "Open the door. I just want to talk."

"Why don't you have any clothes on if all you want to do is talk?"

"Fine," she replied.

I heard footsteps as she walked away from the door and closed my eyes and prayed for her to leave just a little bit more fervently. "Alms for the poor, is that what you want? A life guided by your words and your wisdom? Whatever it is, I'll do it. Just ... please ..."

The footsteps came back towards the door. I sighed and gave up on prayer. "I put my clothes back on, although I really hope you'll agree that won't be necessary in a little bit. Will you open the door so we can talk?"

"We're talking just fine with the door closed."

"James, why are you being so difficult?"

"Difficult?" I gasped. "Difficult? Are you fuckin' kidding me? Do I need to remind you of the broken margarita glass and what you did with the shards? Do I need to remind you of the knives? And what about the months after we broke up when you absolutely wouldn't leave me alone? Difficult? Difficult?" I moved further back into the room, further away from the door, and looked around for any additional barriers I could throw between us. "I think I'm being imminently reasonable."

That's when Beelzebub snuffled up to me. I hadn't noticed he had squeezed into the bedroom before I slammed the door shut. He rested his head on my leg and let his drool drip down. I snuffled a bit back at him. It's a thing I did. Tried to talk to him in his language. Just for the heck of it.

"What was that?" Audra asked.

"Nothing. I was talking to the dog."

"Oh that. Of course." She jiggled the door handle. I thanked the unknown and unnamed god that I had thought to lock it. "How's B doing?"

"He's fine. Just fine."

"I bet he misses me. Just like …"

"No! He doesn't!! And neither do I! Go! Away!"

"James …"

"Leave. Just leave." I stood up and started pacing back and forth. "There's nothing for us to talk about." I stopped pacing and looked at the door. "I mean, seriously, it's been, what, almost 18 months since the last time you pulled shit like this. We haven't talked since. Not a text, a call. Nothing."

"I know. I've missed you."

"Well, guess what, Audra? I have not missed you. Not one single bit. It's been wonderful and peaceful without you in my life."

She was quiet for a moment until the sound of her sniffling came through the door.

"Are you crying?"

"No-o-o-o…"

"Oh, come on. Are you telling me you haven't moved on? Started dating other guys? Surely, you're not still stuck on me."

"I am. I tried. But, you're the one for me and always will be. If I can't be with you, I just can't be."

I heard her get up then and her footsteps trailed away from the door. I knew what this meant. "Audra," I yelled. "Stay away from the god-damn knives."

I went to the door, opened it and raced towards the kitchen. Entering the family room, I was caught short. Audra was leaning against the sofa now. Still without a stitch of clothing on.

And here's where I explain something to you. She had a body men would die for. I, in fact, had once almost died for the sake of her body and the pleasures it offered. But that's a story for a different day.

I stood and looked at her. She wore nothing other than the smile on her face. "Come, James," she beckoned to me, holding her hand out and gesturing for me to approach. "I won't bite."

She might not, but I knew this. As the old cliché goes, every rose has a thorn and Audra was figuratively filled with them and I would not escape unscathed. Yet, I found myself taking a step forward as though she were a magnet and I was just a cheap piece of metal unable to fight the pull.

I took another step before my senses returned. Without a word, I turned to run back to the safe haven of my bedroom and the locked door.

The only problem is that Beelzebub was standing right behind me and I tripped. I'd like to have a video of what happened next because I have no doubt I flew. Awkwardly flailing. Through the air. Before landing on my

73

face with a grunt. I had no time though. I immediately started scrabbling the floor.

"James?"

"Audra is a bitch!" squawked Lucifer.

"Wait. What did he say?"

Before I could respond, Lucifer squawked again. "A real bitch."

I gave up on responding and instead pulled myself up to a crouch, planning on making a lunge forward. "Did you teach him that?" It sounded as though she was right behind me. Her voice rose. "Did you?"

I chanced a glance behind me. Audra hadn't moved. But the smile was gone and she was looking down at her hand as she started to flick her fingers. Those plastic, fake fingernails that made a hideous clacking noise when she drummed them on the table. And now were making a quiet tick, tick as she flicked each finger with her thumb. I knew what this meant. I should have run. I didn't. I stood my ground. I did more than that.

"Actually, yes, I did." The flicking stopped and she lifted her eyes to me. I grinned the grin of a mad man and took a step forward. "Put your damn clothes on and get out of here."

"How could you teach the bird that?"

"I had to teach Lucifer the truth, didn't I?" One more step. "You. Are. A. Bitch."

I could see emotions shift across her face. Anger. Uncertainty. Sadness. I thought she would cry again, although I was thinking the first was a bit of fakery. She wasn't above that, that's for sure.

Audra turned to her clothes draped on the back of the sofa and began to get dressed. "I guess I'll leave, if that's what you really want."

74

"It absolutely is what I want." There was a small piece of me, a corner of my brain that was disappointed at seeing her putting her clothes back on. I wouldn't have minded …. No, stop that. She needed to go. "Please. Leave."

"You don't need to say anything more. I get the message. You don't want me."

"You're right."

Audra picked up her purse and began to walk towards the door. "Do you mind if I get a drink of water before I leave?"

"What? Really?"

"Is that so much to ask?"

"Fine. Get a drink of water."

She changed direction and went into the kitchen, taking a glass from the cupboard and filling it with water. She took a couple of sips before setting the glass down. As I watched her, I realized my mistake a split second before it bloomed into a reality. The knife block was right next to the sink. Audra's eyes were on it the whole time she stood by the sink with her glass of water.

"Audra … don't …"

It was too late. She took the largest knife there was. The butcher knife I got from Cutco a few months before. The thing could slice through meat like it was nothing other than butter. One or two times I had cut a finger while using it and those cuts went deep, leaving scars behind.

"This is new, isn't it?" she asked. Her face was like a stone, whatever light in her eyes had gone out. She ran the flat of the blade along her forearm. "Hmmm…" she practically hummed to herself.

And then she whispered to herself, almost too quiet for me to hear. "James doesn't want me anymore."

"Audra is a bitch," squawked Lucifer. "A real bitch."

***

I guess I need to stop here for a minute and let you know something before I go on.

I'm in jail and ... what I've been doing is writing down the details of what happened. My attorney suggested I do it. To make sure that I don't forget anything. Every detail I can think of because ... here's what happened.

Audra died and, to be honest, I don't know what happened, but they arrested me for her murder. All I know is that there was a lot of blood and that she slipped, or I slipped, or maybe both of us slipped. Beelzebub was there and, I think, maybe one of us tripped over Beelzebub like I did when I was trying to escape from the she-devil.

Something happened. The knife that she was holding and ... just ...that's where I'm at right now and I gotta tell you. I'm really scared. I've been in jail for five days. It wasn't so bad the first few days, but two days ago they put someone else in my cell with me. I haven't slept since because he is a murderer. He shot a couple people in a drive-by and they apparently think it's okay for me to share a cell with this guy because I'm in for murder too.

All I know is that other than telling me what he did, he hasn't said a word to me. Mostly what he does all day long is stare at me, which is what he's doing right now. So I need to keep writing and somewhere along the way I need some sleep. Did I say I haven't got any sleep for the last two days. I can't ... I can't ... I can't close my eyes because I don't know what he'll do if I do.

I'm gonna keep writing this and I'm gonna tell my attorney what happened and, hopefully, somewhere along the way, I'll get out of here before this guy does something to me. I sure hope he doesn't do anything to me.

***

"James, if you don't shut that damn bird up … I will." She moved the knife so the light filtering in through the windows glinted and danced around. Damn, she knew how to handle a knife. Except where it mattered the most. Cooking was not a thing for her. It was something somebody else needed to do.

"You know that truth is a defense." I shrugged. "Besides, you know that once you teach a bird to say something it's almost impossible to get them to stop. So … do what you gotta do."

She started to speak again, but I held my hand up to her. "Shush. Put the knife down and leave. Or I'm calling 911. Lucifer can say whatever he wants. Go. Now."

"No," she screamed. "You listen to me …"

"You're an empty threat, babe. You're not going to do anything with that knife. You never did. All those times. You never did. You're not going to now." I started to walk towards the kitchen. I cursed that there were two ways in and out of the kitchen. One opening by the front door. The other that led into the dining room. As soon as I walked to one end, she started inching towards the other. "Stop. Just put the knife down and leave. Please."

She didn't stop, just kept backing up a step for every step I took forward. As I entered the kitchen, she was at the other end, with a clear shot towards Lucifer. "You don't think I'll do it, do you?" she asked.

"No. You aren't." But I wasn't so sure anymore. Her face was still closed and dark. There was no light there. There was something in her manner I had never seen before.

When I took another step towards her, she raised her voice again. "Stop!" And then she lifted the knife that still rested on her forearm. She angled it so just the edge rested against her skin, and then slowly, lightly moved it along her arm. It was just enough pressure that the damn Cutco knife broke the skin. Blood began to seep from the wound almost immediately. She looked down at what she had done and then looked back at me, her eyes wide. She repeated herself, "Stop!" And then, as the blood began to drip down her arm and begin to drip off her fingertips, she turned and approached Lucifer's cage.

I fumbled for my phone in the pockets of my shorts. It wasn't there. I cursed my lack of a land line, thinking that if I had one, the counter between the kitchen and family room would have been a perfect place for it. The phone would have been right there, but no. I skipped that piece of aging technology and I had apparently left my cell in the bedroom.

"Would you please stop?" I started to plead, not liking the weakness in my voice. "Let me get something to wrap around your arm. We can talk."

She ignored me as she got to the bird cage. "It's too late." First, she reached her bloody hand into the cage and started to stroke Lucifer's neck. "Hey, Lucifer," she whispered.

"Audra is a bitch," the stupid bird squawked.

I watched as Audra tightened her grip on the knife and raised it towards the cage, sliding it in one of the openings and bring it close to Lucifer.

"Stop it, Audra!" I screamed and raced around the other end of the kitchen. As I turned the corner, my foot slipped on the spilled blood and I went down hard. I started to get up, looking at Audra and the bird the whole time.

"No, James. No. It's too late." She moved the blade up to Lucifer's neck. "It was always too late, wasn't it?"

I tried to get up to reach towards Audra. The blood on the floor caused me to slip as I scrabbled up to a standing position, and then I lunged for her. I don't know if it was the blood, or Beelzebub, but I tripped again and as I fell, I could see her move the knife. I heard this strange bizarre squawk from Lucifer.

Audra started to pull the knife from the cage and, as she did so, I reached for her ankle and I yanked her down to the ground and then I heard something else. She screamed a scream like no scream I had ever heard. A scream that was so loud and then it ended in a gurgling, blubbering, wet noise. All I know is that I had my hand on her ankle as she fell to the ground.

I let go and looked at her. Audra was laying on her stomach. I looked up at the birdcage. Lucifer was no more. I moved to Audra's side and turned her over and there was the knife. The big, butcher knife that could cut anything, embedded in her chest and stomach, all the way to the hilt.

There wasn't a lot of blood. Maybe the knife was stopping it or something. I reached down and grabbed the handle and pulled it out and that's when the blood poured out of her.

Audra was still alive, her eyes looking up at me. She tried to say something, but she couldn't. Her lips moved. Her face in a grimace of pain. Her eyes weren't dark anymore. They weren't flat. They were filled with fear. She knew what was going to happen. So did I.

I leaned back against the sofa with the knife in my hand and blood pooling around us. Beelzebub came to me and sat, looking at me with those eyes. Beelzebub sat in the blood that flowed from Audra and waited for something. I don't know what.

I guess I was waiting too. A few minutes later it came. Sirens wailed down the street. It turns out a neighbor had heard the scream and called 911. It was only moments later there was a knocking on the door.

"Police. Open up! We've received a report of a woman screaming. Open up!"

I didn't know what to do. I just yelled, "I think it's unlocked. Come on in."

They did. They came in. They saw a bloody knife in my hand and Audra dead. Beelzebub panting next to me and blood everywhere.

I was arrested immediately. Taken down to the jail. Can I blame them? It makes sense with everything they saw.

I figured though if I told them what really happened, they'd let me go. I tried to but they didn't care. I don't know they were even listening. This was an easy case to them.

They moved me into a jail cell. Days later, I have a public defender who wants to know my side of the story. I've finished writing it down now and I may give it to him tomorrow. But now …

I have to deal with this basic fact. I am not a murderer. I did not kill Audra. No matter what it looked like. And I'm sitting in this cell with a cellmate who is a murderer, who is proud of being a murderer and all he does is stare at me. Unblinking.

I need to get out of here.

Oh wait, hold on a second. He's getting up. He's approaching me. I tried to back up. I tried to melt into the wall, but I couldn't. As he got nearer, I saw he had something in his hand. Something he was rolling back and forth. I wanted to scream for help but my lips, my mouth, everything, was frozen.

He stopped right in front of me and knelt down and held out his hand. I couldn't look. I didn't want to. Maybe if I didn't look it wouldn't happen.

He smiled then and said, "Tootsie Roll."

I looked down in his hand and there was one of those paper-wrapped bits of candy I remember from my childhood. I started to laugh. I couldn't stop. It was all I could do.

Where This Came From: A writer friend published a novel featuring Beelzebub and Lucifer as actual devil-like characters. I don't remember why, but I decided to write a different story featuring Beelzebub and Lucifer and I think the first line of this story came from the Monday evening prompt writing group mentioned earlier.

* * * * *

She sweats
And strains
And hollers it out
"Jesus LOVES You!!"
Between twin tracks
She stands
Tattered bible in hand
"He loves you.
Yes, he does."
She whirls and twirls
Screams Jesus again
He saunters
His sign held out
"Jesus Saves"
And strolls
At the corner
He asks
"Jesus Saves,
Can I get an Amen?"
Screamin' Jesus
Can I get an amen?
He loves you
Yes he does
Who's he love?
The homeless man
Stomping down the street
Grunts and grimaces
Gestures and groans
Evil and hate
Cover his face
Or its demons

Clouding his brain?
Who's he gonna save?
The sunburned man
His hooded eyes
And sideways glare
Walking in endless loops
Cherry red
He leers and grins
Poisoned by drugs
His mind a blank slate?
Screamin' Jesus
Who you gonna save?
Who you gonna love?
Screamin' Jesus?

Coyote

The coyote lurked right at the edge of the yard, where the light from the porch reached that place where the darkness of night overwhelmed the glow. Even at that edge, I could see the reflection in his eyes. Two red orbs that looked back at me every time he whipped his head in my direction. For the most part he didn't do that though. He paced back and forth right at that edge. From one end of the yard to the other. Not looking at me, or at the house. Just straight ahead. To that end. And then turning and jogging back to the other end. Back and forth he went.

I wondered what it was he was waiting for. The last chicken had died months ago. The lambs to the slaughter shortly after that. Wrapping things up before we moved meant there wasn't much livestock left. Moving back to the city can do that.

Dora and I had tried to make a go of country life. Escaping the mad dash of urbanity. We quit our jobs at the health care company where we both worked. After two years, we had yet to figure out a way to make a real go of it. Our savings dwindled, our patience with each other at a breaking point, we caved. Two weeks before, escrow closed on the property, and we had two days left in the country home that we had hoped for so hard. Tails between our legs, we were moving in with her parents until we figured out what was next.

"Hey honey, whatcha doing?" Dora called from the kitchen.

I ignored her. I wasn't sure what she would think about the coyote on the fringe of the yard. I took a seat on the top step of the porch and watched him some more.

"Honey, you out there?"

I could tell her voice was closer. She was coming out.

"I'm just sitting out here, enjoying the night," I finally replied. "The stars are ..."

That's when the screen door wheezed open and Dora stepped on to the porch. "Wow. Look at the moon," she sighed. "Yeah." I looked back at her and patted the step next to me. She was right. It was huge. Round. Full. And lurked just above the horizon, filtered through a few trees. It had just a hint of orange to it as well. If it wasn't for the coyote, that's what I probably would have been looking at.

It was then that the coyote's pacing changed. He stopped and turned his attention to the porch. I felt his eyes bore into me and as Dora sat next to me, the coyote charged. Leaving the comfort of the half dark edge of light, he came across the yard. Straight towards us.

I rose and pulled Dora up with me. "What the hell!" she whispered to me, grabbing my hand.

"Go inside," I screamed and pulled the screen door open, shoving her in. I followed her, and before slamming the front door shut, I took one glance back at the coyote. For the first time, I saw the foam dripping from its jaws, and I could have sworn the animal was smiling at me. Or leering. Or something.

And then I thought about *Cujo*, that Stephen King novel I read when I was a kid. The one that put me in fear of dogs for years. I slammed the door shut, turned the bolt, just as I heard the coyote come up the steps and slam into the screen, setting the springs and hinges to jangling.

Dora and I got a dog a year before. A corgi. At first, I was terrified because I'd never had a dog as a child and there was that damn King story. It only took a few weeks until I realized how foolish I had been. Seriously. Who could be afraid of a corgi? Me.

But I got over it. Ralph, the dog and don't ask, had been shipped to the in-laws the day before. I was thankful for that. Typically, in the evenings he roamed the property before coming in and curling up at the foot of the bed. I can't imagine what the coyote would have done with Ralph if he'd been outside that night. I caught myself with an image in my head. Blood and a dead dog.

* * * * *

I was riding my bike along the trail that winds along the American River and decided to take a rest before turning back into the head wind that always pushed against me when heading back to Sac State. There was a little park tucked along a curve of the trail. Plenty of shade and a couple of picnic tables.

It's where Dora and I met. She was at one of those tables, reading a book. We got married less than a year later. We promised each other a few things that day.

"I promise to love you forever."

"And I do you too," Dora responded. "I promise to be your friend no matter what."

"As do I to you." I looked down at the paper shaking in my hand. "We will grow old together."

"With children and grandchildren."

"And happiness and love."

I held my hand out to her and we danced under the moon that night.

In the months that followed, we were eager to begin fulfilling those promises. It didn't matter if we lived in a small apartment at the time, but six months after the wedding, Dora had her first miscarriage. It took a month or two, but she recovered and we kept on trying.

The second miscarriage, though, took something out of her. I wondered if the hole would ever get plugged again.

Truthfully, the corgi wasn't just for me. To get over my fear of dogs. Cujo!!! No, it was also for her. To give Dora a thing to care for.

86

To love, as she would a baby. Maybe. Maybe she would heal and be whole again. She loved the dog, but it didn't help. Not really. We had started fertility treatments and that was a whole other thing that seemed to suck the life out of her.

* * * * *

It was quiet outside for a moment and then the coyote slammed against the screen door again. It growled. No, it wasn't a growl. It was an unearthly shriek that split the air.

I looked back at Dora. "What do we do?" she said to me, her voice barely above a whisper.

"You stay here. I'm going to get the gun."

"Jack?"

"What else can we do?"

"Call 911?"

"No. I'll take care of this."

We'd bought the gun when we moved in. I thought it was necessary since we were out in the middle of nowhere, but I hadn't fired it in almost the entire two years we had lived there. When I first got it, I shot at old cans on a tree stump back behind the house. But I quickly tired of that, and the gun had been upstairs for too long.

I turned to the stairs and took them three at a time, with Dora pleading, "Just call 911. You don't need to do this," while the damn coyote kept attacking the screen door and splitting the air with its shrieks.

The gun was in a shoe box in our closet, with the clips scattered loosely at the bottom of the box. I reached around in the dark until I found it and then picked the whole thing up and raced back downstairs.

"Here," I handed the box to Dora and ripped the lid off.

"Please just call the police, Jeremiah, please," Dora pleaded. She held the box in one hand and had her phone in the other. "Here. Please."

"No. We need to do this. That thing is rabid. There's no telling what it'll do in the time it takes a deputy to get here." To prove my point, the coyote slammed into the screen door again and I heard the screen clatter as it fell to the porch floor. The next charge was straight into the door. It didn't seem like anything was going to stop the beast.

"You're not going to shoot that thing!" Dora screamed this at me, but she also held the box out to me while I reached in for the gun. "You can't do that, can you? Shoot an animal?"

I fumbled in the box for a clip and dropped it to the floor before I slammed another into the heel of the gun. I grabbed a second clip, putting it in my pocket and dropping the box to the floor.

"Honey, please. That thing isn't going to be able to get through the door."

I noticed that the coyote had stopped, that it was silent on the other side of the door. Maybe I wouldn't need the gun, and then I heard the growl. Followed by a shriek, and instead of slamming into the door again, the coyote went at the window next to the door. The window shattered and the coyote's head was in the house. It's red eyes darted around. Foam, mixed with fresh blood beginning to ooze from cuts on its snout, dripped to the floor.

* * * * *

Back when we were making promises to each other, I made a few of my own.

"I promise to keep you safe and to protect you." I said this to Dora when I proposed to her. Back at the bench in the park along the American River where we first met. "If you will marry me, I promise to always be there for you, to slay your demons, and bring light into your world."

You see, Dora had some issues. I learned about them late at night, when the world was dark and quiet. Occasionally, Dora wasn't so quiet. In her sleep, she would cry and yell. When she did, I'd reach out and hold her until she calmed down. In the mornings that followed, she would tell me of her nightmares. Some of them were actual dreams. Some weren't. Some were all too real memories of her past. I meant to protect her from all of them.

That morning when I proposed to her, Cora cried for a bit before she accepted my proposal. She wrapped her arms around my neck and breathed into my ear, "Yes, oh definitely, yes."

For a time her night terrors seemed to pass. Maybe, the mere fact that I had committed to her forever had eased her fears. For months we were happy, there was definitely light in our lives.

We rode together along the bike trail, we ate breakfast in bed, and stayed up late playing cribbage and nuzzling each other as we slept through the night. After the first miscarriage, something changed. I'm not sure she slept more than a few hours for the next three or four days. She called in sick at work. "Babe, I just need some time," she told me, when I suggested we get away together. "By myself. You go to work."

I did, because I wasn't sure what else to do. This was a thing I wasn't prepared for. My wife mourning a child that never was. And when she finally was able to sleep, she began to cry in her sleep again. All I could do was hold her.

When she got pregnant again, things were better. Until they weren't and the second miscarriage came almost immediately after we got the good news. I learned then that my promise was empty. I couldn't protect her from everything. There were some demons that couldn't be slayed, and all I could do was watch and catch her if she fell too far.

*****

But this, this damn coyote, this was something I could save her from. I had a gun and a clip, a spare in my pocket. The coyote wasn't going to get any further.

That's when it shrieked again — an ear-splitting, unholy sound that ripped through the air. And I dropped the gun, while the coyote pushed further through the shattered window.

"Jeremiah!" came another shriek from behind me.

"Go upstairs. To our bedroom. Shut the door and move something in front of the door. Barricade yourself in there."

"I'm calling 911."

"Fine." I bent down, not taking my eyes off the coyote, and felt around for the gun. "Just do it from upstairs."

As Dora turned and walked upstairs, I mumbled to her, "They won't get here in time."

After what felt like three hours of groping for the gun, while the coyote growled and spit and Dora slammed the bedroom door, I finally looked away from the threat and looked down. It was right there, in the one spot I hadn't reached. I grabbed it and held it in both hands, turning it on the coyote.

I was breathing hard, my hands were shaking. I looked at the red eyes and bloody snout and tried to calm down. If I pulled the trigger right then, there was no telling where the bullet would end up. I needed everything to stop. Just for a few seconds. To get my breath under control, to steady my hands, and to convince myself to do it.

Dora was right. I couldn't shoot it. It sounds stupid, but … I closed my eyes on the beast and counted backwards from ten. It was a trick my mom taught me when I was a kid. To calm myself whenever I was feeling nervous or scared.

10 …

The coyote growled from deep down its throat.

9 ...

I could hear Dora pushing the dresser across the floor of our bedroom.

8 ...

Breathe in, breathe out.

7 ...

I thought of the one ultrasound we had, from the first pregnancy. There was a little peanut growing inside of Dora's body. It was ours.

6 ...

More glass broke off from the window, clattering to the floor. I wanted to open my eyes. I didn't.

5 ...

Breathe in, breathe out.

4 ...

Dora yelled down to me, "I've got 911 on now."

3 ...

Steady hands. Steady.

2 ...

The coyote shrieked again.

Breathe in, breathe out.

Steady. Steady.

1 ...

I felt hot breath on me.

I opened my eyes and fired, and missed wildly. The bullet shattered a window on the other side of the door, but the blast from the gun at least stopped the coyote and set my ears to ringing so loudly I couldn't hear a thing.

From behind me, two arms reached around me and grabbed onto my wrists. "You've got this," Dora whispered in my ear.

I pointed the gun at the coyote, my wife steadied my hands. We waited to see what the thing would do. When it growled again and lifted its red eyes to leer at us, I pulled the trigger.

"We got it," I whispered to Dora as I dropped the gun to the floor.

Where This Came From: I don't remember what the prompt was, but I believe this came from the Monday evening writing prompt group. Much more than we typically write in the 20-30 minutes we have to write during our scheduled sessions. But once I started this one, I wanted to see it through to an end.

* * * * *

I want to
I want
I
I want
I want to
Words of such power
Words of such weakness
Words that speak
Words that breathe
Is a want a need
Is a want a desire
Is a want something more
Is a want even real
I want to
Love
Laugh
Cry
Feel
I want to
Feel the wind
Feel the sun
Feel the waves
I want to
Feel your touch
Feel your warmth
Feel you
I want to
Walk the world
Swim its rivers
Share its rhythms
I want to
Talk to you
See you smile
Hold you tight
I want to

Spaces After the Period

When we first met I wasn't so impressed. I had always gone for the prototypical bad boy. Tattoos and wild hair, leather jackets and a Harley, nonchalance and indifference. I hardly knew how to act when you were so nice to me. Holding a door open, offering your hand to help me out of the car. In those initial moments, though, all I could see was the physical you. Two inches shorter than me. Hair already thinning. And a button down shirt.

I couldn't believe my sister thought we could be right for each other. And when you started talking about your mother's corned beef, it was all I could do to stifle a yawn and claim an impending illness to cut the night short. Something held me back. I gave it a shot. I gave you a shot. This strange thing happened by the end of the night. After dinner, while we walked along the river, you slipped your hand into mine. Suddenly, it was just there. And it was warm. And right. No man had ever held my hand before. Not like that. All those Zachs and Codys and, yeah, Joe, my god, Joe. They held my hand in the throes of mind-blowing sex. It is one thing those tattooed losers have going for themselves.

But they never held my hand just to hold it. To provide comfort. And you did. I didn't even realize I needed it until that night. It was one of those things you taught me, usually without a word or gesture. It was the way you were. The way you could just touch me and I could then see things in a way I had never seen them before.

I should have run that first night. I mean, seriously. You, a quiet Jew, who was comfortable with your G-d. Me, a snarling and assertive atheist, scornful of believers in anything. See what I did there, I spelled it your way. To honor you.

You were eight years older than me. All those bad boys had been, always, younger. Some of them barely legal.

You had a job. I had art. You paid your bills. I didn't know how much mine were.

You were an anchor. I was a kite.

So we walked and we talked. At the end of the night, we parted ways. I went back to my apartment where I would have to move the drop cloths and dried brushes to find a place to sleep. You, back home to your mother. I shuddered when you told me that, but your hand was still in mine so I couldn't go far.

When you pulled lightly and brought me closer to you, I almost laughed as you closed your eyes and brought your face to mine. There was something about your innocence and purity that sucked me closer while screaming at me to flee. The peck on my cheek, not on my lips, that first night, oddly kept the screams at bay.

I cursed my sister for what she had gotten me into. What horrible misfortune was going to befall me if I saw you again? Would I be sucked into a world of quiet dinners with the folks, afternoons at the symphony, and semi-expensive sedans that I would have laughed at in my prior life?

You called me the next day, but I couldn't find the phone so you left a message. "Ummm. Hello, this is Mitch. Mitchell Steinbaum. Ummm … I was just calling to say hello and thank you for a wonderful evening. Ummm … I'll call you later?"

I never deleted that message and I listen to it now when I need to hear your voice. I still laugh, even through the tears that are falling, that you had to tell me your full name. As though I had gone out with more than one Mitch the night before. It was that uncertainty and the uncomfortable hesitation in your voice that pulled me even closer.

I thought about waiting for your call, but I couldn't. We talked again while I lay in my apartment eyeing the wall of white where only the week before I had begun to apply the colors of a falling sun, and you pushed paper across your desk while filling my head with your words. Hours passed.

And then days. And weeks. And months.

We didn't see each other again for five days and by the time we did, I ached. I couldn't' believe it. How you had wormed your way into me with such simple, small gestures. I cursed my sister again. I called her and asked her what the hell she was thinking. She just laughed and said, "I knew it." By the time you picked me up, I felt like the lone survivor of a shipwreck, rescued after days of hunger and thirst.

Halfway through our second date, you fed me your line. Only I knew it wasn't a line. For you it was the truth and it was heartfelt. Dinner was wrapping up, there was only another swallow of wine left in our glasses, our dishes had been cleared, the bill had been paid, and you leaned forward. "You know, we're like the two spaces after a period."

"What?" I leaned forward too, bringing our faces perilously close. "What are you talking about?"

"You and me. We could be like those spaces. You know, a sentence ends with a period and there are two spaces. We're those two spaces waiting for the next sentence to begin."

I laughed then. "But there's only one space after a period." I couldn't help it. You said it so earnestly, I needed to make a joke. So early and so unexpectedly, you committed to the idea of the two of us, being a connection in the midst of a story. Inside, I took a breath and thought maybe, just maybe. I decided to see what the next sentence said. I held you with my eyes and leaned further in, but this time I closed my eyes first. I tasted the sweetness of the wine on your lips and the gentleness that was you.

I never ever wanted to be one space again.

We began the next sentence that night, but as with everything it was slow and quiet and respectful. You were always a gentleman. There was no rush. No expectations. Nothing other than letting the words of our story flow naturally and as they would. When we parted ways again, you left me at my apartment door with a hug that swallowed me into your world, letting me know that there was much more than a single sentence in our future.

You taught me to love the symphony. I only fell asleep during a performance once. I strapped you into a raft for a trip down the rapids. You didn't scream. Much.

You admired my falling sun, while perched gingerly in the only clear spot on the edge of my sofa. I fell in love with your mother. Over corned beef and cabbage – and yes, it was excellent – I saw how much you loved her.

Just like a man can look at a woman's mother to see what she might be like in thirty years, I say to see how a man will treat his wife, look at how he treats his mother. A man who cared for his mother as you did could only be a blessing for a girl like me.

Our sentences began to flow out and form our story. Painstakingly, we began to weave images and memories that created our slow-building tale. I have no doubt an outsider looking in, a reader of our imaginary sentences, might have been bored. Mightily so. But, it was the pace and delay, the anticipation that built, the sense of rightness that was what we were becoming that made it all work. We were writing our story and not racing to the end to meet another's objectives.

Then your mother died. You cried in my arms the way men do. Even you could not let it out easily. You shuddered and fought your tears, before letting them fall in a river of pain finally released. And that night, we made love. For the first time.

Your fingers along my neck. Your hands on my breasts. Your hot breath on my skin. The intensity of your eyes as you stared deeply into mine. How you quietly took all of me in and then released me. It all left me feeling at the end like I had been handcrafted just for you. You molded me and formed me that night and I had never, ever felt love as pure and deep.

If there was any doubt before, it was gone. In the quiet night that followed, with your arms around me, I felt complete.

We began to speak of things like a home. Together. You never suggested I move in with you because your mother was gone. Instead, with your first words, you said what was necessary. "Let's find a home for both of us. An office for me. It doesn't need to be big. But we need white walls everywhere."

"Why?" I asked.

"For you to paint," you laughed. "And plenty of cans of white paint in the garage for when you want to start over."

"I love you," I replied and you held me closer. I didn't need the words from you. I knew. Your actions. Your touch. Everything about you told me all I needed to know about how you felt.

You sold your mother's home.

We found a little place down by the beach. Two bedrooms. One for us. One for you. Vaulted ceilings that provided for grand walls for me to work. And a breakfast nook that looked out over the ocean. Whenever we needed a moment, that's where we would meet. With the ocean crashing on the rocks below, we could talk. Or not. Deep conservations about our pasts or about our future. Deeper silences when we might sit side by side, the table pushed back and our chairs facing the windows. Your feet up on the sill. My head on your shoulder and my legs curled under me. We would sit and watch. Uncountable moments would pass with nothing more than the sounds of our breath, the beating of our hearts, and the quiet rush of time passing by.

There was this moment one day when I began to wonder whether that was it. Our simple life. You, with your job and the bills paid faithfully each month. Me, I had those walls and I had you. We had the ocean and we had time. Was that it?

That night, while we watched the falling sun as it disappeared beyond the ocean's edge, you pulled me to you and, quietly, you asked, "Will you marry me?"

"Well, duh." I slugged you in the shoulder, my nagging doubts dissipated with the beauty of those four simple words. "What took you so long?"

And so it was. You promised to be mine. I promised to be yours. Our union was blessed by the State and by your G-d. I didn't need any of it. But I did. We had our home. We had our view. We had our hands entwined and words of love. We had the words and sentences that continued to tell our story. Somewhere along the way, it had come time to start a new chapter. You knew it and turned the page. Thank you. For always knowing when it was time to wait and when moving forward was needed.

You know, though, that sometimes the pages turn and new chapters begin without your control.

We were going along, comfortable with our lives and with each other. You gave me my space while holding me close. I'll never know how you could do it. One day I realized something had changed. I went to the drug store. I went to the doctor. And then I waited in the nook for you to come home. On my cell phone, I listened to that old voice mail and began to cry. Tears of joy at the thought that we would soon become three spaces after the period. With a whole new story to tell.

Where This Came From: A good friend called me one day to complain about a boss who kept removing the extra space she put in between sentences in documents she wrote for her job. I agreed with her. It's always been two spaces after the period and we bemoaned the perils of modernization. For some reason, that conversation gave me the idea for this story. It's one of my favorites.

* * * * *

The words, they come slower
The days, they go faster

As time goes by
Change is constant
As time dwindles
Nothing changes

A time, when all seemed possible
A past, where possibilities died

Memories of things
That never happened
People once loved
Love that crashed

The words, they come slower
The days, they go faster

Waterfalls stream
Rainbows shimmer
Days darken
Nights creep

Of friends, many remembered
Of others, mostly forgotten

Love was a thing
Beauty inspired
Light my life
Memories fade

The words, they come slower
The days, they go faster

Deviation

"What should I do?" Mickey furrowed his brow. "Get the usual, I guess."

"Nah, break out of the rut, man. No cheeseburger tonight."

"Yeah, a little deviation never hurt no one, did it?"

"Exactly. A little deviation is good for the soul." Johnny laughed. "You know, like maybe you should try your shit on a brunette tonight instead of a blonde. De-vi-ate from the norm." Johnny slapped his hand down on the table and laughed again.

"What can I get for you two?" Ally asked, her pencil already scratching something on her order pad.

"You first," Mickey said.

"Me first. It's always me first. For somebody who never deviates, why can't you make up your damn mind?" Johnny tossed his menu to the table. "I'll get an omelet with home fries, cup of coffee, mushrooms and onions on the omelet."

When the pencil stopped scratching along the pad, Ally turned to Mickey. "I'll get ... the ... cheeseburger. With bacon!"

"Woohoo! Adding bacon. Now that's a deviation."

Mickey watched Ally walk away before turning to Johnny. "Why do you gotta be so negative? Shouldn't a brother be more supportive?"

"All I'm doing is trying to get you to expand your horizons. A brother should challenge and motivate. Even a little brother."

"Why do you care if I get a cheeseburger?"

Johnny sighed. His cell phone, on the table in front of him, vibrated. "It's not just the cheeseburger. You know that." Johnny checked the phone. "Shit." He typed a message. "It's everything. You get the cheeseburger here. The fish tacos at Isabella's."

"So what …"

"Mickey, it's not just the food. How many years you been wearing nothing but black Converse high tops?"

"I like 'em."

"Yeah, but you even wore them to Steph's wedding, man. That wasn't cool." Johnny's phone buzzed again. He looked at the screen and quickly typed another message.

"What's going on?" Mickey asked.

"Nuthin'." Johnny looked out the window before turning back to Mickey. His eyes watered. "Mom's in jail again."

"Shit." Mickey slumped back against the seat. "Again?"

The waitress stopped by to top off their coffee.

"What'd she do this time?"

"Same as always. Maybe that's where you get it from. She's got no deviation." Johnny took a sip of his freshened cup. "Damn, that's hot!"

"Yeah, maybe you should blow on it next time."

Johnny waved his hand at Mickey. "Where's the challenge in that?"

They sat silently for a moment. Johnny sipping carefully. Mickey twirling a knife. "Well …?" Mickey asked, not taking his eyes from the flashing light of the knife.

"Oh, yeah. She was out there peddling her god again. Out on K Street. That old man got in her face again."

"What's his name? John? John Dempsey? What's Mom call him? Mumblin' John?"

103

"Yeah. Him." Johnny put his hand over Mickey's and stopped the twirling knife. "Stop that. It drives me f'in' crazy." Mickey put the knife down and began drumming his fingers on the table. Johnny cocked an eyebrow. "She decked him. Knocked him to the ground."

"Damn."

Johnny's phone vibrated again. He checked the message and chuckled.

"What's so funny?" Mickey asked.

"She used her Bible."

"What do you mean?"

"She hit him with it."

"No shit!" Mickey stopped drumming his fingers and looked at the phone in his brother's hand. "Who's texting you all this anyway?"

"Dad."

Mickey pulled his own phone out and looked at it. "Why ain't he texting me?"

Johnny stopped mid-chuckle. "You know why."

"No, I don't. Why?"

Johnny looked out the window again, wiping his hand through his hair. "'Cause he knows that my love for our mother outweighs yours."

"Fuck no," Mickey yelled. Philip and Gertrude, the old couple at the corner table, looked up and shook their heads before returning to their egg creams. Ally started to walk over before Johnny waved her away.

"Take it easy, man. You know it's true."

"Fuck no," Mickey whispered, staring intently at his brother.

"When was the last time you got her a card for her birthday?"

It burst out of him like a volcano erupting. A guffaw Mickey directed at his brother. "That's the problem with you and Dad. You equate a card with love." Mickey began flipping the knife over and over again. When Johnny looked at him, Mickey returned his glare but kept flipping the knife. "You ever get a call from Mom in the middle of the night? You ever have to hold her when she cries on your shoulder because Dad hit her again?"

"Dad hits Mom?"

"Exactly. You think you've passed the test because of your cards and because you sit with her now and then. And Dad with his stupid flowers and chocolates on Valentine's Day."

"Dad hits Mom?"

"No shit, Sherlock. Yes, Dad hits Mom! What's Hallmark got to say about that? Huh? Dad hits Mom."

Johnny sipped his coffee, ignoring the heat. "How long have you known?"

Mickey scratched his chin. "I've always known, man."

Ally wandered over and refilled their water glasses, the clinking of ice drawing Mickey's attention. "Thanks, Ally," he mumbled, noticing the chipped red polish on her nails and the absence of a ring on her left hand. Before she walked away, he cast his eyes up at her and smiled. She was a redhead. Maybe his brother was on to something about that whole deviating thing.

"You're welcome," she responded and turned to walk away. Mickey watched her go, her hips sliding loosely in the tan waitress's outfit she wore.

"I don't know how you couldn't know," Mickey said, his eyes still on Ally. There was something about her he had never noticed before. She had a subtle beauty that didn't scream to him in the neon glow of so many other women of his generation. Her hair was simple, not swept up. Her make-up was minimal, except for that red polish.

105

And she never raised her voice. She was quiet. Subtle. And not a blonde.

"What do you think?" Mickey flicked his eyes at Ally.

Johnny turned to look at her, giving her a head to toe scan. He shrugged, "I'd do her."

"Damn, Johnny. Really?"

"What?" Johnny looked back at his brother. "Oh, wait a sec. You in love, man?"

"No." He twirled the knife faster. "I'm just ... you know ... she's not a blonde."

"Yeah. A redhead. That's way more dangerous than adding bacon to your cheeseburger." Johnny slid to the end of his seat and leaned back, his head against the window, and closed his eyes.

They were silent for a moment or two before Johnny opened one eye to peek over at his brother. "A redhead, huh? Looks like you may actually be cutting the ol' umbilical cord." Johnny sat up again and faced his brother. "Tell me about the Mom I don't know about."

"I can't"

"Why not?"

"She made me swear I'd never tell you."

"What..."

"Didn't think you could handle it."

" ... the fuck?" Johnny cried out. In the corner, Phillip and Gertrude shook their heads again and hurried to finish their meal, celebrating the day 52 years before when he proposed at the very same table. "What the hell does that mean?"

"Oh, come on. You melt down at the slightest thing."

"Do not."

"Uh … yeah."

Ally brought their food to the table, interrupting them. "Hey," Mickey said, as she placed their plates on the table. "Thanks."

"No problem," she replied with a smile.

"Nice one. 'Hey' all cool and smooth." Johnny took a stab at his omelet and crammed a bite into his mouth. "You better up your game, buddy."

"Knock it off."

They chewed in silence for a moment, a silence broken by the clattering of forks on plates, a whispered conversation from the corner table, and Ally taking an order two tables over.

"So, you're telling me the Humane Society President beats his wife?"

Mickey began to pick at his bun, nipping at the outer crust, revealing the lighter interior. "Dammit, Johnny."

"What?"

"She made me promise."

"You gotta be kidding me. You can't tell me about my own dad beating our mother? They're my parents, too."

"Fine." Mickey pushed his plate to the side, the burger barely touched. "You remember a few years ago? They had a barbecue and Mom came out in a long sleeve shirt. At one point, she stood up to reach for a plate of food, her top rode up a little, enough to reveal a kaleidoscope of bruises on her stomach." Mickey pulled a fry from his plate and chomped at it. "You remember that?"

"No."

"Of course not. You probably thought nothing of her wearing long sleeves in July either. But I know you saw it. We looked at each other after she sat back down. You let it go. I didn't." Mickey let the hint of accusation linger for a moment.

"Everything okay here?" Ally asked.

"Yeah …" Mickey began.

"Good. Let me know if I can get you anything else."

"… but you're fuckin' irresistible," Mickey finished to the retreating figure of the latest girl of his dreams.

"You know, if you told her that to her face, instead of mumbling it to yourself, you might actually get a little something. She might be just the kind of girl who wants to know a loser like you finds her irresistible and likes a little f-bomb thrown in there now and then."

"Fuck you," Mickey mumbled.

"Fuck me?" Johnny repeated in mock amazement.

"Yeah, f-u-c-k you."

"You're a joke, you know that?"

"Whatever." Mickey pulled his plate back and began to pick at the fries, selecting out the crispiest and nibbling them like a rabbit going after a carrot.

Over in the corner, Phillip and Gertrude rose from their seats. The remnants of their anniversary meal a scramble of plates and empty glasses, crumpled napkins and a 15% tip. To the penny

"You two," Gertrude said, approaching the table Johnny and Mickey sat at. Her husband stood by her side, grimacing. Behind her, Ally approached with a coffee pot in hand.

"Hush now, dear," Phillip said. His hand on her elbow, trying to guide his lifelong companion past the brothers.

"Don't you be shushing me, Phillip," Gertrude replied, pulling her arm away from his guiding hand. "I've got something to say and I'm gonna say it."

She stood at their table, Phillip behind her right shoulder shaking his head. "You boys got it all figured out, don't you?"

"Ma'am?" Mickey spluttered.

"You two sit here with your foul-mouths talking about her," Gertrude slanted her head towards Ally, "like she's … like she's not even human. And you think …"

"Honey," Phillip tried one last time.

"Now, you shush," Gertrude said over her shoulder at her husband of all those years, before turning back to Mickey and Johnny. "You two, you're a self-fulfilling prophecy. You know that, don't you? You sit here, bitch and moan and get nothing."

"Excuse me," Johnny said.

"Oh, now you're polite because an old lady is standing in front of you. What about a few minutes ago, when you were dropping your 'fuck this' and 'fuck that' like a sniper with a hair trigger? Firing off your … oh what do the kids call it … f-bombs, that's it … like there's no tomorrow."

"Gertrude?!?!" Phillip returned his hand to her elbow. "We really must be going. Come dear." To Mickey and Johnny, he said quietly, "Alzheimer's. Please forgive her."

Mickey spotted the tears forming in the corners of the old man's eyes as he spoke. He said all that he could think of, "It's not the Alzheimer's. She's right, you know. She's right."

"Ms. Wiecks, let's get you to your car." Ally stepped in, and, with Phillip, began to direct her towards the door.

"Damn. Crazy old woman," Johnny muttered.

"That's just it. You don't get it. Why Dad beats Mom. What that old lady was talking about."

"What are you talking about?"

"Damn, Johnny, you're simple. You say I need to deviate to expand my horizons." Mickey picked up his mangled burger and took a bite, chomping on the cold meat and drying bun. "You know what it is? It's this. There's this world out there you don't have a clue about.

"Yeah, I gotta deviate. A brunette instead of a blonde. I gotta up my game if I want to get a little action from the hot waitress."

"Mickey …"

"Shut up for a minute, wouldya?"

"Fine." Johnny slumped back against his seat. "Shoot."

"There's a whole frontier out there you know nothing about. It's the line between pain and love, suffering and happiness. Anger and joy, and hate and help. It's that old woman who hears us 'fucking this' and 'fucking that' and it sends her up the wall. It's not her god-damn Alzheimer's. It's the pain of hearing the utter lack of respect in our voices and our words."

"When did you get so damn philosophical?"

"It's not philosophy, Johnny. It's real life. We sit here every Friday night. Not deviating." Mickey held up his hand to stop Johnny's interruption. "Yes, you don't deviate any more than I do. It's Friday night and what are you doing? Having dinner with your brother at a greasy spoon. How long we been doing this? Not deviating on a Friday night? We're, like, in this world that ain't real, you know. Talking about this and whining about that.

"My god. You don't even know Dad hits Mom." Mickey stopped and looked at his brother. Johnny wouldn't make eye contact. "Although I think you've always known, too. You just chose, instead of dealing with it, to try to ignore it. To bury it. Well, guess what, big brother. Life, real life, is unyielding.

"You'd do Ally, would you? But, you don't know the first thing about her." Again, Mickey held his hand up. "I'm not criticizing you. I'm no better."

Johnny sighed, "You take this shit too seriously, you know that? I was joking about Ally."

110

"Really? Like you were joking about Jessica? And Diane? Sylvia? How you'd do them? Like I was joking when I said Ally was f'in irresistible? And, what about last month, when that chick walked by in the short skirt and the red heels? We looked at each other and said 'damn!' like we'd won the lottery or something, for a woman we didn't even talk to, let alone touch."

They were interrupted by the door opening and Ally stepping back inside after helping Phillip guide Gertrude to their car. She glanced over at Mickey, caught his eye and smiled. He smiled back and for a moment was lost in the sparkle of her eyes and the sway of her hips, again, as she turned towards customers sitting at the far end of the diner.

"Mickey?"

"Mickey?"

"I've got an idea, Johnny."

"What's that?"

"Let's start with a thimbleful, nothing more. Respect."

Mickey stopped when he saw tears beginning to form in the corners of his brother's eyes and then begin their stroll down his cheeks.

"I knew," Johnny said.

"What?"

The tears turned to sobs as Johnny continued, "I knew Dad hit her. How could I miss it?"

"Johnny."

"But, I didn't know it, you know what I mean?" Johnny's voice hitched as he gathered a breath. He motioned to Ally to take his plate away. "When I realized, really knew, what was happening … I don't know, I just figured it was too late. Better to ignore it and put a happy face on things than to say 'hey, Ma, what's with the bruises?' If

I ignored it, maybe Mom would find comfort with me. You know what I mean?"

Mickey slurped his soda and scarfed a cold French fry. "Yeah, I do."

"It's time, isn't it?" Johnny asked.

Mickey looked up as Ally approached. "I think you're right. We have a mission, don't we?"

"More than one, wouldn't you say?"

"How you two doing over here?" Ally asked.

"A simple overture?" Mickey asked his brother, his eyebrows raised, a smile forming.

Johnny wiped his eyes and sniffled. "Yeah. Fuck yeah. An overture."

Mickey turned to the subtly beautiful waitress standing at the end of their table. A wisp of hair leaked out over her left ear. Small dark circles shadowed her eyes. "On behalf of …"

"No, Mickey, let me do it," Johnny interrupted.

"Ally, my brother and I would like to apologize to you for our behavior tonight."

"What are you talking about?"

"Well … uh … our language and disrespect."

Mickey intervened. "Ally, we're sorry. And, I'd like to make it up to you."

"What's wrong with your language?"

"Well, you know …"

Ally leaned over and whispered in Mickey's ear. "You turn me on. If you whisper something dirty to me right now, I guarantee I'll do anything …" Ally licked her lips quickly, barely brushing Mickey's ear with the tip of her tongue as she did so. "… anything you want."

"Well …" Mickey said, his face turning red and a line of sweat beads forming along his hairline. "Who can quibble with that? I mean who can fuckin' quibble with that?"

"Yeah," Ally whispered in Mickey's ear.

Mickey looked questioningly at his brother, the moisture in his eyes still there.

"Damn," Mickey sighed, turning to face Ally. "How do you feel about a rain check?"

Ally stood up quickly. "What do you mean?"

"I've got something I need to handle here now. How about later? When do you get off?" Mickey pleaded with his eyes and reached out to touch her arm with a fingertip.

As though a door slammed shut between them, Ally's face changed. The smile gone, her eyes like steel. "Can I clear your plates for you?" she asked turning her focus to a spot between Johnny and Mickey.

"Uh, sure." Johnny pushed his plate towards Ally who piled it on Mickey's and turned quickly away from the table. "What just happened?"

"Nuthin'."

"Mickey?"

"Ummmm …" Mickey cast his eyes down to the table and began to twist a corner of his napkin. "I think … I don't know." He looked up at his brother. "Fuck it. I just feel like there's too much to juggle right now."

"What are you talking about?"

Mickey leaned over the table to whisper to his brother. "She said she'd do anything I wanted."

"Damn! And you said 'later'?"

"Johnny ... I just, I don't know ... I mean, Mom's in jail. We gotta talk about her and Dad. And ... well ... damn, Ally is cute, but ... I'm juggling things here."

"Don't say it, Mickey, don't you dare say it."

"She ain't blonde."

"My god, you have got to be fuckin' kidding me. She'd probably blow you in the parking lot right now and you can't get past her fucking hair color." Johnny slammed his hand down on the table and began laughing. "I can't believe you."

"Yeah. You can't believe me." Mickey stared at Johnny. "You know what your problem is?"

"My problem," Johnny chuckled, "is that I've got a fucking knucklehead for a brother."

Mickey crumpled up his napkin and flung it at Johnny. "No. Your problem is that your ignorance is so wide ... so widespread, it hides you from the real world."

"What are you talking about?"

"Let me try again," Mickey picked up the salt shaker and shook a few grains out. "These are the problems that exist in your world." He flicked a grain towards Johnny. "That's what you eat each day." He flicked another. "That's when you go to sleep." And another. "That's whether you're gonna get any this weekend." And the last. "That's whether you're gonna call Mom and talk to her about nothing that matters."

Mickey unscrewed the top from the salt shaker and poured out its contents. "And this, this represents the problems that everybody else has to deal with." Mickey swiped at his hair and shuddered. "I can't even begin to index them all. Love. Heartache. Pain. Suffering. That my father beats my mother and there ... is ... absolutely ... nothing I can do about it." Mickey slammed his hand on the table with each word before settling back with a sigh. "Except listen to her cries late at night when he's finally fallen asleep."

"Mickey …"

"And the little things. The pleasure in clouds and the fright of a thunderstorm. The unruly discomfort at being lost finding the place you wanted to stop for a burger. And being lost in your life's mission." Mickey stopped and smacked his forehead. "Oh, wait, that's right. Your life doesn't have a mission."

"Enough," Johnny interrupted.

"Who do you care about? What do you care about? Even more importantly than any of that …" Mickey stopped and lasered in on his brother. "Do you even care?"

Johnny looked over his shoulder before leaning forward and motioning for Mickey to lean in. When their foreheads were almost touching, he asked, "Don't you want to get laid?"

"Aw, fuck." Mickey exclaimed, leaning away from his brother.

"That's it, isn't it? You're afraid." Johnny was whispering, leaning as far forward as he could. "The pressure of it all, right? You've got this hot little waitress you've been eyeballing all these months, you finally say the words tonight and she tickles your ear with words you're too afraid to hear."

"Johnny … I'm trying to get at something a little more important than …"

"You can't just put a piece of bacon on her and say you're deviating, can you?"

"Shut up."

"Shut up? That's the best you can do?" Johnny leaned back and slapped his hands. "I've got an idea." Johnny turned around and motioned to Ally.

"What are you doing?"

115

"Don't worry, Mickey. I got you covered."

"Can I get you anything else?" Ally asked, turned towards Johnny as though he were the only person at the table.

"Um, yeah. I've got a question for you."

"Johnny?"

He held his hand out to Mickey to shush him before continuing. "You ever consider dying your hair a different color? You know, maybe try being a blonde?"

Ally's eyes narrowed a bit while Mickey slumped down, happy for the invisible wall she had erected between them. "I'll get you your check." Ally strode away.

"What the fuck do you think you're doing?" Mickey asked, beginning to draw a line through the pile of salt.

"Trying to save you from yourself."

"Really? All I can see is you're a massive liability."

Johnny laughed. "Liability? Me? No, you're your own liability. So wrapped up in whatever it is going inside that head of yours you can't even live."

"You know what, Johnny?"

"What?"

"Fuck you." With a swipe of his hand, Mickey swept the pile at his brother, covering his shirt in a layer of scattered salt.

Johnny looked at the layer of salt and smiled. "Good one."

"Yeah," Mickey chuckled. "I just covered you with my problems."

"Really?" Johnny mused. "If one of your problems is carrying on some torrid kind of thing with Ally, I'll take it. I'll whisper sweet f-bombs in her ear," Johnny leered, "all night long."

116

"You're a punk. A fuckin' punk, you know that?"

"Yeah? So what? Who always gets laid?"

"Fine. You get laid. I'll go see what's going on with Mom."

"Oooh. That's low."

"It's reality, Johnny. You go buy your card and get laid. I'll take care of our mother."

Ally returned to their table and laid the check down. "Whenever you're ready with that," she said, before twirling on her heel and walking away.

Mickey's eyes followed Ally's hips. Johnny, swiveling to watch her go, followed her legs.

"Damn, why didn't I notice her before?" Johnny mused, finally starting to brush the salt off his chest. "I'd love to run my hands up ..."

"Johnny."

"Yeah. Never mind. Maybe I'll just talk to her about it later tonight."

"Can you do me a favor?"

"Yeah, what's that?" Johnny turned back to Mickey.

"Go fly yourself a fuckin' kite."

"Yeah, right." Johnny picked up the check. "Is it my week or your week?"

"What's the date?" Mickey sighed.

"Uh. 17th?"

"Yeah. Odd dates are yours. Even are mine."

"Oh, yeah. That's right."

"That's right? You act like we've never talked about this. Shit."

"Damn, Mickey, what the hell is your problem tonight?"

Mickey took the check from Johnny and looked at it. He reached into his pocket and pulled out a wad of bills. He began to count them out. "No problem. No problem at all."

"Why are you paying the bill? It's my day, isn't it?"

"Yeah. It's your fin day, but you couldn't just pay the bill without asking, could you?" Mickey motioned to Ally and laid the bill with the cash on top at the end of the table.

"I'll get your change."

"No. That's it."

As Ally picked up the money, Johnny reached out and touched her wrist with his finger. When she looked at him, Johnny motioned with his eyes. Ally leaned towards him. "Closer," he said to her. She leaned in closer. "Tell you what, you take care of our check there, and then come on outside. We can huddle up in the parking lot and I'll say whatever you want."

Johnny leaned back with a smile that said the world was his oyster and waited. Ally stood up straight and fiddled with the cash in her hand. "You two. Damn, I don't know what to do with you." She turned to Mickey. "You, well, you turn me on. With all of your earnestness and need." Ally looked back at Johnny. "And you, well, you're just an ass."

Mickey began laughing. Ally turned back to him. "I wouldn't laugh if I were you. A girl can only wait so long, you know. I've got certain needs and if you aren't gonna take care of them, well I may just have to settle for the ass, if you know what I mean."

Ally walked away with their payment, Johnny's bravado, and Mickey's uncertainty in the palm of her hand. Johnny took a sip of his coffee, now cold, and watched Mickey from over the rim of his cup. Mickey fiddled with the one remaining napkin on the table, ripping it slowly into tiny shreds.

"You know. I think it's time to avenge our mother's suffering." Mickey looked sideways at his brother, just seeing him out of the corner of his vision.

"But ..."

"Johnny. Here's your chance. Prove you're better than you really are. Fuck Ally."

"Well, actually ..."

"No, I mean, forget about her. It's time to do the right thing instead of the pleasure thing."

Johnny sighed. "You're probably right. Damn." Johnny's eyes begged as he continued. "I don't suppose there's time for a little parking lot quickie?"

"No."

"No?"

"No."

"Damn. You sure?"

"Johnny?"

"Fine. What's your plan?"

"Well, first thing is that you've gotta erase the blackboard."

"Huh?"

"God, you are so fucking dense." Mickey shook his head. "You've got to wipe your memory of what you think about Mom and Dad. You need to refurbish your parent memories and start over. Clean them off and be ready to replace them with something else."

"What's that?"

"Reality."

"Shit."

"You gotta do it, man. You know. Start realizing there's a whole lot more salt in the shaker."

"Cut it out."

"What?"

"With the salt. Damn, I'm probably going to be sucking salt out of my belly button for weeks."

"You or this month's girl?"

"I could hope."

"You could. What's her name anyway?"

Johnny paused. "Ally?"

"Ummm ... no. How 'bout we agree that she's off limits for you?"

"Fine."

They were silent for a few minutes, while they chewed on their thoughts. Johnny broke the silence with a tentative approach.

"How often did he?"

Mickey sighed and reached out his hand as though he wanted to physically connect to his brother before he responded, but contact wasn't made as his hand fell to the table with a thud. "I don't know. I suppose if I tried, I could chronicle the times Mom told me. Or I figured it out myself.

"You know ... the barbecue. Her birthday a couple of years ago when she didn't want us to do anything for her." Mickey began to trace circles on the table. "Back when we still lived at home, how many times did she stay in her room and tell us to make dinner for ourselves 'and make sure you put something together for your father,' she would say. My blood boiled when she would make sure he was taken care of even while she licked her wounds."

"You knew in high school?"

"Of course I did. The question is how the fuck did you miss it?"

"I ..."

"Don't bother, Johnny." Mickey held his hand up to shut Johnny up. "It's water under the bridge. I know why you didn't know then but there's no point in re-hashing that. The question is whether you're ready to do something about it now."

"What do you think we oughta do?"

"What I shoulda done years ago. Go home and save her from him."

"How are we gonna do that?"

"Don't matter."

"What do you mean?"

"It's that question that has held me back all these years. How do I go about doing it? Well, that's not an issue anymore. We're just gonna do it and figure out the details as we go."

Johnny brushed a few last specks of salt off his shirt and looked up at his brother. If Mickey had to guess, he might have thought there was a little more moisture in his brother's eyes than usual. "Yeah, let's fuckin' do it. If nothin' else, we can kick the son of a bitch out and lock the door behind him."

Mickey and Johnny rose from their seats. As they left Billy's Diner, the door closing quietly behind them, Mickey turned to his brother. "You know what?"

"Huh?"

Mickey rubbed his stomach. "I'm not sure that bacon was such a good idea. I'm not feeling so good. It's like ... like there's a brouhaha going on in my gut."

"Yeah?

Mickey groaned and rubbed his stomach again.

121

Johnny laughed. "So much for deviation. I've heard redheads don't go down so well either."

"You're a flippin' freak."

"Yeah, I'm a freak. And, you need to lighten up. Damn, these Friday get-togethers used to be enjoyable. Talking about girls and shit. But, you got all your philosophizing and serious thoughts going on in your head. It ain't so fun anymore." Johnny turned back to Mickey, who remained by the entrance, the lights above casting his face in an eerie shadow. "Damn. You even look like death." Johnny shook his head and continued towards his car.

Mickey didn't move. He only raised his voice. "What's wrong with being serious, Johnny? You think life is just fun and games." He paused for a moment and then lowered his voice. "Tell that to Mom."

Johnny stopped in mid-stride and spun around facing his brother across fifteen feet of parking lot asphalt. "What was that?"

"You heard me."

"No, actually. I didn't. I think you said something about our mother. I just want to make sure I got it right."

"Drop it." Mickey started walking, brushing by Johnny. "Let's go."

Johnny followed along, mumbling to himself, "What did he say?"

They got in Johnny's car, a blue Gran Torino. With the rumble of the engine coming to life and a puff of smoke out of the exhaust pipe, they were off.

"Did Dad bail her out yet?" Mickey asked.

"No. He says he's not going to either."

"Why the hell not?"

"He said in his last text, and I quote, 'I'm tired of her god shit.'"

Mickey started hitting his head against the head rest behind him. "That is so fucked up. It is entirely out of proportion. He beats her up, keeps her hidden away for days while she heals and every once in a while she gets out and wants to share her love of Jesus with others and …

"You got to admit she's a little overboard with it."

"Really? You think she's overboard with her religion?"

"Yeah. She gets a little crazy with it sometimes." They pulled up to a red light. The car rumbled beneath them. Johnny pulled his pack of cigarettes from the dashboard, tapped one out and lit it.

Mickey sighed and opened his window. "If you're gonna smoke, could you open your window, too? You know I hate the smell."

Johnny grumbled but complied. "Don't you think it's weird that the Bible is the only book she reads?"

"Weird to you, maybe. But maybe that's where she finds solace in a life like hers. Ever look at it that way?" Mickey coughed, not because he needed to. "Mom finds a little bit of peace in those words. They comfort her. Why does that have to be weird?"

Johnny looked at the cigarette in his fingers, grimaced and flicked it out the car window. "I'm done with these."

"Thank you!" Mickey exclaimed, slapping the dashboard with his hand. "You can donate the money you spend on cigarettes to a women's shelter."

"What? No way. I'm gonna spend it on Ally."

"Johnny, we had a deal."

"Fuckin' relax, Mickey. I was just kidding. It is so easy to get a rise out of you."

They rode in silence for a moment before Johnny broke it. "Where we headed?"

"What do you mean?"

"I don't know. Go home and kick dad's ass or head to the jail and try to get Mom out?" They pulled to a stop at another red light. Straight meant the jail. Left meant home. Right meant indecision.

Mickey drummed his fingers on the arm rest. "We gotta get Mom out of jail." He looked over at his brother. "Don't we? We can kick the old man's ass later." Johnny laughed, a sound barely audible above the rumble of the Torino's engine.

"You got any money for bail?"

"Oh. Yeah. That could be a problem. Do you remember how much it was last time?"

Johnny grimaced and thought about it as the cross traffic light switched to yellow. "No. Dad took care of it then." Their light flicked green. "What do we do?"

Mickey looked at the traffic in the lane next to them begin to move past and looked back at the car behind, it's headlights glaring, the right one brighter than the left. He turned back as the driver tapped his horn. "You know, my anger has grown exponentially, but I'm not ready for him yet. Let's get to the jail and find out about bail." The driver behind them leaned on his horn again.

Johnny began to inch the car out into the intersection. "You sure?"

"Yeah. Let's get this mess over with. First Mom and then we take care of him." Mickey slapped his hand on the arm rest and bounced in his seat. "I need my anger to coalesce a bit. You know?"

Johnny laughed again. "No. I have absolutely no idea what the fuck you're talking about. Anger coalescing? Shit."

"Never mind."

Mickey looked out the window as they rode in silence. In the jail's parking lot, Johnny shook out another cigarette. "What?" he whined, looking at Mickey before his brother could say anything. "Just one more. I'll be quick."

"Yeah," Mickey sighed, settling back in his seat. "You criticize me for not being able to deviate, but you got your habits, too, you know."

"Smoking ain't like only dating blonde chicks."

"Why not?"

"Smoking's a disease. It's a fucking addiction."

"Maybe I'm addicted to blondes. You ever think of that?" Mickey laughed. "Maybe there's an intoxicating scent that emanates from blonde hair that does something to my brain chemistry."

"Shit." Johnny opened his door, dropping his cigarette to the ground and smudging it out with the heel of his shoe. "Let's go."

Inside, the desk sergeant laughed. "You mean the Bible thumper who practiced her pugilistic arts on John Dempsey?"

"Hey, that's our mother you're talking about." Johnny's voice raised a notch.

"Yeah?" The sergeant's face darkened. "She gave a beat down to a bum."

"What are you talking about?" And it went up another notch. "She just bumped him on the head with her Bible."

The sergeant chuckled and pulled a file out of the middle of the stack in front of him. "Let's see. The perpetrator was one Emily Anne Santini." He looked over his granny glasses. "That your mother?"

"Yes," Mickey and Johnny replied in unison.

"According to the first officer on the scene, the aforementioned Ms. Santini was found to be standing over Mr. Dempsey, yelling at him, 'you better find God, Mumblin' John, or a whole lot more shit will be raining down upon your soul.'" The sergeant began to close the file. "And that's when things got a bit more serious."

125

"What? What happened?" Mickey asked. "Wait a sec. Our mother wouldn't have said that."

Ignoring him, the sergeant went on. "A crowd had gathered, refusing to disperse at the officer's request. He had to call for reinforcements as the crowd chanted to Ms. Santini for more. The officer retreated to his car and pulled out a beanbag gun and fired it several times into the crowed. Meanwhile Ms. Santini leaned over the unconscious Mr. Dempsey. She thumbed through her Bible, finding a page she wanted, turned the book over and placed it over the man's face."

The sergeant leaned back. "That about do it for you gentlemen?" Before they could respond, he slapped his hand down on the desk and jerked upright again. "Hold on a sec. There was something else you might find interesting." He opened the file and thumbed through a few pages. "Here it is. The page she left the Bible open to had the following passage underlined. Matthew 25:35. 'For I was hungry and you gave me food, I was thirsty and you gave me drink, I was a stranger and you welcomed me …' What do you make of that?"

"Wow," Johnny muttered. "I've got no fuckin' clue."

"Of course, you don't," Mickey mumbled back. "Your mind is so scantily clad with the shreds of intelligence, you can't possibly understand."

"Fuck you."

"Yeah, fuck you, too."

"Ummm. Boys," the sergeant intervened.

Mickey ignored him. "Johnny, it's a cry for help. Don't you get it? She's hungry and needs to be fed. Your cards mean jack shit to her. She's thirsty in the middle of a desert. Dad's flowers and chocolates on his good days don't carry over to the bad. She is utterly lost and feels unwelcome in her own world. God, I sometimes

126

wonder if one of us was adopted. You absolutely cannot be my brother."

"I ... I ... I ...," Johnny stuttered, before turning to the sergeant, waving off his brother. "What's her bail?"

"She hasn't been arraigned yet, son."

"What the hell does that mean?"

"It means," Mickey answered before the sergeant could. "Bail hasn't been set."

"What?"

"Damn, don't you watch cop shows?"

"Yeah. I love Law and Order."

"Learn anything from them?" Mickey looked at the sergeant with sorrow-filled eyes. "Standard protocol is bail isn't set until the arraignment, am I right?"

"Yes, you are."

"Well, when the hell is that gonna happen?" Johnny demanded.

"Probably Monday. That's the problem with getting arrested on a Friday night."

"Fuck that. She's stuck in here over the weekend and there's nothing we can do?"

The sergeant suddenly could only focus on the file before him. "Ummm. Yeah." He looked back up at Johnny. "Sorry."

Johnny looked at Mickey and then back at the sergeant before returning his gaze to his brother again. His eyes teared up. "Mickey? What are we gonna do? We gotta get Mom out of here. This sucks."

Mickey reached out to hug his brother. "It does," he whispered in Johnny's ears. "But let's go take care of that other thing then. We'll get her out on Monday after they set bail and make sure he's long gone before she gets home."

"All weekend, Mickey. All fuckin' weekend."

"I know."

"Maybe she should conduct her street preaching earlier in the week," the sergeant offered with a smile.

Before Mickey could stop him, Johnny exploded, "Maybe you should shut the fuck up! That's my mother you're talking about." The heads of officers scattered around the station snapped in their direction while the desk sergeant popped out of his chair.

"Johnny, let's get out of here. Come on." Mickey pulled at the sleeve of Johnny's jacket, chiding him quietly as they backed towards the entrance to the police station, "You need to keep that temper in check. Now is not the time …"

"I don't give a fuck. That little desk pimp talking about Mom like that with that little smirk on his face." Johnny halfheartedly tried to pull away from his brother before he realized that it wasn't just the desk sergeant who had a hand on a gun holstered to a hip.

"Yeah. I know," Mickey whispered in Johnny's ears. "But, don't worry. He'll get his some day too. It's all about karma, you know."

Johnny whipped around and faced his brother. "Would you cut it out with that shit? Damn Mickey, with your salt shaker theory, making overtures, and now this karma crap. Here's a novel idea for you, my philosopher king brother. Zip it!" He took a step closer and started jabbing his finger in Mickey's chest. "Now … is … not … the … time. I don't need your shit."

Mickey swatted his hand away and reached to wrap his arm across Johnny's shoulders. "Let's go, Johnny. Save this rage for Dad. Whatever you do, make sure you keep your ass in a pucker until we get home."

"Your brother's advice is something you oughta listen to." Behind them stood an officer. His name tag said Riley. Officer Riley was a small mountain of a man with a barrel chest and forearms equal to Mickey's thighs. He stretched his arms out and put his hands together, cracking his knuckles before swinging his arms back to rest loosely at his sides. Johnny's temper cooled considerably as the brothers beat a hasty retreat to their car.

Silence filled the Torino for a few minutes until Mickey broke it. "You hear anything more from Dad?"

"Nope."

"Damn."

"Yeah."

"You think he knows?"

"What?"

"That we're coming for him?"

Johnny looked over at Mickey and scoffed, "How could he know?"

"Don't know. It just seems like he's always been one step ahead. You know?" Mickey laughed. "It's like ... I wouldn't be surprised if he's got a sentry or two posted at the house. Or maybe a booby trap. I don't know. I can't help feeling like he knows."

"How could he know?" Johnny repeated.

"Do you remember that Christmas when we peeked under their bed and saw what our presents were before they wrapped them?"

"Yeah. That was cool."

"No, it wasn't. What happened after we opened our presents Christmas morning?"

Johnny's voice darkened. "He took them away from us and gave them to charity."

"Yes. And why did he do that?"

"He knew."

"Exactly!" Mickey exclaimed. "He fuckin' knew just by the looks on our faces that we had cheated Santa Claus. That is exactly what I'm talking about. He knows things he shouldn't know."

"Oh, come on, Mickey. That's different. We were little punks and we probably reacted differently than he was used to and he put two and two together

"What about when you took his Mustang and headed to Tahoe for a couple of hours while he and Mom were in the City celebrating their anniversary?" Mickey held his finger up to prevent Johnny's explanation. "You even figured out how to roll the odometer back before you left and washed the car before he got home."

"You know how dad was about that car. He probably noticed it was parked an inch farther into the garage than he left it."

"No. That's not it. He knew. There's something I never told you about."

They were entering the neighborhood now. The squeal of the tires as Johnny took the turn too fast slicing through the night air. "What's that?"

"He called home while you were gone."

"So."

"He asked me where you were."

"So." Johnny's voice hinted at his exasperation. "He always did that to check up on us. Make sure everything was okay."

"No. This was different. Before I even said hello, he blurted it out. 'Where's your brother?'"

That stopped Johnny cold. He made the left that took them further into the neighborhood. Only another left, followed by a right, and a half mile down, and he'd be pulling the Torino to the curb in front of the family home. "Fuck."

"Yeah. Fuck."

"What'd you tell him?"

"First I panicked." Mickey began to giggle and couldn't stop until they were almost there. Through his laughter and tears, Mickey continued, "I couldn't think of anything and he asked if I was still there. So I told him you were in the shower, jacking off."

Johnny snorted, snot flying from his nose as he joined his brother, laughing until he cried. "What'd he say?"

"You're not going to believe it."

"Shit. I already don't."

"He said, and I quote because I'll never forget it, 'Better requisition that boy some lotion and Kleenex,' and then he hung up."

Johnny pulled over, three houses short of their goal. The Torino was slanted across the curb, the right front end cutting a diagonal slash across the sidewalk, almost nosing into the evergreen bush that lined the Simpson's front yard.

"He said that?"

"Yes."

"Our dad? Joe Santini, the fuckin' Humane Society President who beats his wife?" Johnny chuckled one last time. "Always thought he was kind of a prude, you know?"

"I guess there are a lot of things you're learning about the ol' family dynamic today."

Johnny pulled the keys out of the ignition and pocketed them. "Yep. I was a sucker for the fairy tale. Maybe you're right about all of this."

"About what?"

"Don't get dense on me now, my philosopher king. Karma and overtures and life being about more than getting laid and eating in the same diner every Friday night. No matter how hot Ally may be."

131

Johnny opened his door and stretched one leg out of the car. "You know, you're not the only one who's been eyeballin' her."

"Johnny …"

"Don't worry, brother, she's yours if you want her. I'll keep my hands off. But I hope you won't mind if I use my imagination every now and then."

"As long as that's all you use."

"Mickey, she's yours. It's a brother's promise."

Mickey looked over at Johnny.

"Oh, dammit, don't fuckin' cry," Johnny exclaimed when he saw the sparkle of moisture in his brother's eyes.

"It's just that you've never made a promise like that." Mickey reached out his hand and placed it on Johnny's shoulder. "I mean, a brother's promise is one of the deepest kinds of promise a man can make to another. It's like …"

"Oh, would you just shut the fuck up." Johnny wrenched himself out of the car and stood up. "Whatever happened to the whimsical brother I had? Once upon a time." Johnny slammed the door shut. "Come on. Let's get this the fuck over."

Mickey wiped the tears from his face before exiting the car. As the dome light winked out, he hurtled the evergreen bush and caught up to Johnny. "What are we going to do?"

"I don't know. Kill the SOB?"

"We can't do that."

"Why not?"

"You want to spend the rest of your days in prison. Your imagination is all you'd have then. That and some Mexican gang member's dick up your ass."

"Yeah, well, maybe we can provoke him and make him strike first and we could claim self-defense."

"Really, Johnny, you wanna kill him? I thought we were just going to scare him and get him to leave so Mom can come home and live in peace. He is responsible for you existing in this world after all."

"Maybe." Johnny quickened his stride as they approached the home where they grew up. "Don't you ever wonder about that, though?" Suddenly, he stopped and turned back to Mickey.

"Seriously. What if we're all interchangeable. Yeah, Dad planted his seed and I came along and you came along. What if," and here Johnny paused and looked to the stars winking in the night before turning back to Mickey, "what if it's all just a lottery? What if he hadn't and I was born to some Sherpa in Nepal and you were born to a cocoa farmer in Colombia? You ever think of that, huh? What kind of karma is that? What kind of cosmic roll of the dice determines our fate?"

"Wow, Johnny, I've never thought of that, but that's ... like ... well, just ... wow!"

"Yeah, it is. It just came to me, too, but here's the deal. We've got no time for this cosmic shit." Johnny turned back toward the family home. They stood at the edge of the lawn, perfectly manicured. The rose bushes pruned, the whites and pinks providing a faint anchor in the dark. Johnny could smell the tangerines from the tree in the corner. Just starting to ripen. None of it mattered though. "Right now I want him to suffer for everything he's done. I want him to feel the pain he's inflicted on her. I want him to believe it should be him in that jail this weekend instead of her. I want to make a fuckin' overture to him that he'll never forget. Not like the one you wanted to make that old crazy lady back at the diner. That was far too polite. No." Johnny began walking slowly across the lawn, his brother tracking his steps, afraid if he stepped anywhere other than where Johnny placed his feet, there would be imbalance in their approach. "I want our father to pay for everything he has done to her. And more. I want to see him plead and beg and cry for forgiveness. And when he does, I want to scream in his face 'Fuck no! You get none from us.' And when he leaves, never to return, I want his tail between his legs and to see him slinking away under a shroud of shame and horror for all that he's done. You got a problem with that, brother o' mine?"

Mickey opened his mouth. "No. Wait a sec." Johnny stopped again and reached his finger out and crossed his brother's lips with it. "Ssssh." When Mickey had closed his mouth, Johnny slowly pulled his finger away, ready to replace it if he tried to talk again. "Here's the deal. If you have any doubts, go back and wait in the car. I'll take care of it. I'm the one who bought into the fairy tale. You never did. I envy you for that. If you want, you can keep your hands clean. Mine have been dirtied already with all that I've ignored." Johnny's voice hitched and caught. "I'm as dirty as he is for ignoring it for all these years."

"Oh, come on, Johnny, you're not responsible. How could you be?"

"Because you were right. I knew, but I opted for ignorance over responsibility."

"So what? It's not like you ever hit her."

Johnny let loose a deep sigh that reached to the winking stars and returned with a quite echo. "I might as well have." He moved forward again, his feet reaching the cement path that led to the front door. "It's time to make things right."

"Let's go then. It's pretty clear you aren't vacillating," Mickey said.

"No vacillation here," Johnny agreed. "Just absolute, stone cold determination."

"Did you hold on to some of that rage from the police station?"

"Got it in vast stores and ready to burn through it."

"Let's go." Mickey stepped ahead of his brother and led the way to the front door. He knocked. Once. Twice. Three times. Through the door, came the scrabbling of toenails on the hardwood floor and then the low growl the poodle let loose from the opposite side of the solid oak panel that stood between them and the tornado that awaited.

"Quiet down, Ruffles," their father said from the other side of the door. "It's the boys."

Mickey's eyes widened. "See. He knows," he whispered.

Johnny slapped his shoulder with the back of his hand. "Dimwit. There's a peephole," Johnny whispered back.

The door creaked open. "Mickey. Johnny. Have you come to discuss what we're going to do about your mother?" Joe started to step out on to the porch. The boys could hear the quiet tinkling of a piano coming from the back room where the baby grand occupied a corner.

"No, Dad. Actually, we're here to make an overture," Mickey began. "To you."

"What?"

"Yeah, Dad. We're here to make a fuckin' overture." Like a snake that has been coiled for too long, Johnny sprung across the entry with his hand stretched out, reaching for his father's neck. To latch on to it and slam him back against the wall. "To you. You mother-fucker!!"

There was a crack as Joe's head slammed against the textured wall, right next to the family picture, taken at Mickey's high school graduation. Mickey in his cap and gown, parents smiling, Johnny facing the camera, but his eyes elsewhere. In the background, the piano ended with a harsh clanging of keys. Johnny lifted his eyebrows. "Who the hell is playing the piano?"

His face turning red, their father grunted and gargled a response before pointing a finger at Johnny's hand that was slowly closing off his windpipe. Johnny loosened it. "Please, boys. Let's talk outside."

Mickey didn't hear him. He was already on his way further into the house. "No, Dad," Johnny growled. "I think we'll head to the back room." He flipped Joe around and shoved him after Mickey.

"Boys. Please."

"Shut up," Johnny order. "We have a lot to talk about and I have this feeling the list just got a bit longer."

Mickey came to a sudden stop, his father running into his back, propelling him into the sparsely furnished room. The piano was the center piece. A couple of chairs and a small coffee table in a corner provided a place to sit. "What the ...!" he exclaimed, turning back to his father and pushing him against the wall. Bringing his right fist back, Mickey held him there. "What the hell is going on, Dad?"

ll Johnny could muster was an emphatic "Wow." He slumped to the two steps that led into the room.

Four scantily clad girls -- women maybe, it was unclear – stared back. The piano player was topless, her perky breasts like the dots at the bottom of the exclamation points the evening had produced.

"Please, son. Drop your fist. Let me explain."

"What do you think, Johnny?"

"Wow. I mean, just … wow."

"Yeah, I know. But, could you rip your eyes off the flesh in this room for just a moment and help me out here?"

"Brother o' mine, I'm having real problems with this. I mean look at those. I could seriously be devoted to her for life." He pointed at the piano player. "Or, wait … her." And he pointed to a girl in the brown leather chair, who sat with her legs crossed, leaning back, wearing hardly anything but a lacy thong and matching bra. In her hand she held a glass of red wine and her eyes had the sleepy look of somebody who just might have had a pull or two on a joint recently. "What's your name?"

"Cecilia," she coyly replied.

"Mickey. Johnny. This isn't what it looks like," Joe interrupted.

"At the moment, I'm totally fine with what it looks like," Johnny told his father before turning back to the creature on the leather chair. "Damn. Cecilia. I'm Johnny."

"Johnny!!!" Mickey roared.

"What? You are seriously getting annoying."

"Did you forget about the overture?" Mickey pushed his father harder into the wall and was grateful to get a wince from him. "How about you deviate a bit from the norm and forget about what you see in front of you and focus on what needs to be done. Remember? For Mom?"

"Boys," Joe pleaded.

Johnny sighed. "Do it."

Mickey rocked his fist forward, connecting with his father's nose, feeling the crunch under his assault. Joe sagged a bit, but Mickey held him steady. "That's for Mom," Mickey screamed into his face, spittle flying, before doing it again, feeling something else in his father's face collapse. "That is, too." He let him go then and as his father slid to the ground Mickey brought a knee up and hammered it into his gut. "For Mom!"

His father lay in a silent heap. "Get me away from this asshole," Mickey said to his brother. "Or I'll fuckin' kill him!"

"Now?"

"Yeah. Now." Mickey began to prod their father with his foot. "I'm pretty sure if you don't I'm going to kick him. I'd really rather not get his blood on my Converses."

Johnny stood up and pushed Mickey gently away. "I got a better idea. Step back for a sec. I'll take care of it." Johnny grabbed their father under his arms and pulled him up with a grunt. "Come on, old man, let's get you out of here. Find you a place to sleep this off." As he dragged him out of the room, Johnny paused for a second. "You surprise me," he said to Mickey. "I didn't think you had it in you. It's inexplicable really. I had all this rage in me and ..." He readjusted his hold. "... it ended up you who let it out. Damn. You did good, philosopher king."

"I don't know that I'll ever be proud of this moment, Johnny."

"Pride? You gotta have pride for this? Why? Just enjoy the moment. Save it to tell your grandkids some day." Johnny dropped his voice into an old man voice. "Let me tell you kids about the day I coldcocked your great-grandfather in a room full of whores." He laughed as he began to disappear through the doorway, father in tow. "But for now, why don't you mingle a bit. You get first choice." His laughter echoed in the quiet hallway. "I got an idea for you," he yelled back to Mickey.

"What's that?" Mickey chuckled, knowing what was coming.

"Deviate!"

"Okay." Mickey turned to face the bounty that awaited. "Girls. Ladies. How about you get dressed and get out of here?"

"We're not going anywhere until we get paid." It was Cecilia, of course. Standing now and striding towards Mickey. He couldn't help but notice she was a blonde, with perfect breasts, a slender waist, hips he could ski off of, and a tattoo along one of those hips. He couldn't make it out until she had stopped in front of him. *The Pleasure Is All Mine* it read in a multi-colored ink. With red hearts on both ends.

"That's nice," he said, pointing to the tat.

"Thank you," she purred. "Now, about us leaving."

"Yeah. You need to go. My father has made a tremendous mistake. He's married, you know."

138

"No shit. We're not here to develop a relationship with him. We're here to provide a service. One he hasn't paid for yet." She placed her hands on Mickey's shoulders and winked at him. "Besides, this isn't the first time I've been here."

"Johnnnnyyyyyy!!!!!!!!!"

"I'll be there in a minute," Johnny yelled from somewhere in the house.

Mickey tried to take a step back from Cecilia. "Why'd you have to be blonde? Why?" He stepped back towards her, leaning in. She smelled of cinnamon and spice and everything nice. Mickey's breathing became labored. Sweat began to bead on his forehead. "I … I … can I touch you?"

Cecilia stood on her tiptoes and brought her mouth close to Mickey's ear. "I want you to," she whispered, her hot breath creating a stir. "The pleasure would," she licked her lips, "be all mine." Mickey reached his hands out to her waist and slid them around to her ass bringing her to him.

"Dammit! Mickey!!" Johnny yelled from the doorway, two bottles of Stella in his hands. "I told you to deviate. If you're not going to, then fuck it. Get out," he roared

From Cecilia's incredible embrace, Mickey responded, "You can't make me leave."

"Not you. Them. All of them. Get out!"

Mickey cast a skeptical eye over Cecilia's shoulder at his brother. "Really? You're throwing this all away because I chose the blonde?" His hands continued to move along her smooth skin

Johnny handed his brother a beer. "Here."

"Not right now. My hands are kind of full."

"Take it."

"Fine." He let go of the girl and took the beer. "Now what?"

"They leave."

"Pay us first," Cecilia demanded.

"I ain't paying you nothing, babe."

"Then ... we ... don't ... leave." Cecilia walked over to where a pile of clothing had been left between the chairs. She began rummaging through it until she pulled out a cell phone. "And I call Tomas."

"Who's Tomas?" Mickey asked.

"Their pimp," Johnny answered before Cecilia could. "Don't call him. I think I have an idea." He held his finger out to her. "Hold on a sec."

Johnny pulled Mickey out of the room. "Here's what I think. We complete the overthrow."

"What are you talking about?"

"Let's find Dad's checkbook and write them a check for twice what he owes them for ... for ... ugh ... I can't even say what he was paying them for." He took a deep drink of his beer. "It's hard enough thinking of Mom and Dad doing it, but Dad with four hookers? Are you fucking kidding me?" Johnny shivered like death had traveled up his spine.

"And here's the added bonus. That's how we'll pay to get Mom out when they set bail on Monday."

"I get it. Yeah. Let's use his money instead of ours. Or hers. That would be beautifully ironic, don't you think? In the process of kicking his ass and kicking him out of his house and Mom's life, we raid his account for her Get Out of Jail Free card." Mickey stopped, his mouth forming a circle of surprise.

"What is it?"

"You want more irony?"

"Shoot."

"Well, we're going to write a check on his account and make them leave, right?"

"Yeah. We got to do it. Don't we?"

"No, actually, we don't. That's where the irony comes in." Mickey laughed and pounded his brother on the shoulder. From the back room, the tinkling of the piano returned. "He's ... wherever you put him. Probably going to be out for a few hours at least. If we're paying them anyway shouldn't we enjoy the fruit of this golden opportunity? Let's go fuck our brains out." Mickey drained his beer and tossed the bottle aside. "That's where the irony really lies. We get laid and he pays for it. Double."

"I'm liking the way you're thinking, but here's the thing. I'm not backing down on this. You've got to deviate. No Cecilia for you. I think you should delve a bit into the mysteries and magic of the chick playing the piano."

"Uh-uh."

"Uh-uh?"

"Let me have Cecilia and you can have the rest. All of them."

"Mickey, you amaze me with your charity. This time and only this time, I will overlook that you are once again unwilling to deviate. Of course, it helps that you're allowing me to engage in a most desired form of deviant behavior. But know this ... oh hell, never mind. How can I say no to your offer?" Johnny finished his beer and tossed it to join Mickey's empty. "Let's go."

"Girls, girls, girls," Johnny announced as they re-entered the back room. "Please accept my apologies for that bit of a digression. My brother and I have discussed this dilemma we find ourselves in. We agree that you should be paid for your services. We're willing to pay double what our father was obligated to pay." He smiled then and shrugged his shoulders. "However, if you get paid it must follow that you should also serve. Am I right?" he asked Cecilia, an eyebrow raised.

"As I said," she purred once again, "the pleasure would be all mine."

"Great. Just great." Johnny began walking towards the piano before stopping and raising his finger in the air. "I forgot." He turned back to Mickey. "Could you go tie Dad up just in case he wakes sooner than we think? He's in the guest room. You can take Cecilia with you. Maybe fuck her there with him in the same room."

"Absolutely not."

Cecilia sauntered towards Mickey and slid her body up to his. "Why not? I think that might just be the hottest fuck I've ever had. Especially if you keep your Converses on."

"Maybe I can be persuaded," Mickey mused.

Hours later, the brothers woke bleary-eyed to the sound of their father yelling at the top of his lungs in a nasally voice they had never heard before. Mickey and Johnny gathered at the door of the guest room.

"What do you think? Let him suffer a bit more?" Johnny asked.

Mickey shook his head. "No. I want this over with. Let's get him out of here, clean the place up and go visit Mom."

"Your call." Johnny opened the door.

The room was dark, lit only by sunlight coming in through the slats of the closed blinds. It smelled of sweat and blood. "Good morning, Dad," Johnny said.

"What'th going on, boyth," he replied. "Why am I tied up?" Joe wheezed in a breath or two.

"Oh, where to start, where to start?" Mickey replied.

"Lithen. If thith ith about the hookerth, I can ethplain."

"Dad, save your breath. It's not about the hookers." Johnny said.

"Although that certainly helps explain a few things," Mickey interrupted. "I think. Johnny, I'm confused now. Does it explain anything at all?"

"Yes, in fact it does." Johnny turned the ceiling light on and watched his father blink his eyes furiously. "Well done with the tying up, Mickey." Joe Santini was stretched as far as he could be. One hand tied to each of the bedposts at the head of the bed and one foot to each post at the foot. "Tell us, Dad, what does it explain," Johnny asked solicitously.

"It, well, you know," he stuttered in reply. "I have needth."

"Hold on a sec, father of ours," Mickey said. "Just so you understand something. The hookers aren't why I damaged your face as I did. I'd like to be sorry for the broken nose and busted teeth, but I'm not. Can you imagine why?"

"Boyth, could you untie me? At leatht?"

Johnny looked over at Mickey and shrugged. "What do you think?"

"Nah," Mickey replied. "Let's wait until we get it all out. For full disclosure."

"Yeah. Full disclosure. I like that."

"What the hell are you talking about?"

"Let's talk about Mom." Mickey pulled the desk chair over to the side of the bed and turned it around so he could rest his head on the back of the chair. "Mom. You know the woman you married all those years ago. You see, your hookers, they actually are just a transitory diversion from the real reason you're in the position you're in."

"Hold on a sec," Johnny said, winking at his brother. "Hookers? There were hookers here?" He slapped his forehead. "Oh … yeah … four of them, right?"

"Uh-huh."

"And, which one did you do? What was her name? Cecilia?"

"Yes, I did indeed do Cecilia and she was incredible."

"Boyth."

"What about you, Johnny? How was the piano player with her perky titties?" Mickey asked. "And the other two? Was it worth the bacteria you probably picked up? I mean, with three of them, your odds of infection expand exponentially, you know."

"Mickey?" Joe pleaded.

"Brother o' mine, Mr. Philosopher King, it was most definitely worth the risk." Johnny slapped his brother on the back. "But next time you have to promise me you'll deviate. Please, man, you just have got to deviate."

"Johnny?" Their father began to sob quietly. "Pleath thtop thith."

"You think we should tell him?"

"Yeah. He'll find out soon enough."

"Dad," Mickey began. "We'd like to thank you for the little gift you left us. We have needs as well and they were fulfilled in the last few hours. I hope you won't mind that we paid for their services with a check from your check book." Mickey stopped and began to untie the rope that held their father's left foot in place. "Oh, and we doubled their normal fee. We thought it might be the Christian thing to do."

Joe began to kick his free leg a bit, twisting and turning against his other bindings. "Boyth, why are you doing thith to me? Why?"

Johnny moved over to untie the rope on his right hand. "Why? How can you possibly ask that?"

"Johnny, thurely you underthtand." Joe flexed his freed wrist. "I'm a man. Your mother ith … well, thee'th not right in the head.

144

Hathn't been in a long time." Their father shook his head. "You know we haven't …"

"Enough!" Mickey slammed his hand down on the nightstand. Joe flinched. "Let's dissect the problem here. Maybe we should use tweezers to pull back each individual layer because it is most definitely a multi-layered dilemma we have."

Johnny sat down on the edge of the bed. "I like that Mickey. Tweezers. Let's begin peeling 'em back. How long you been beating her?"

"What are you talking about?"

Johnny just raised his eyebrows and continued, "How often do you have the hookers over?

"Firtht time. I thwear."

"They certainly seemed familiar with the place and with you."

He slumped back on the bed. "Fine. They've been here before."

"Hey Mickey, you know what I wonder." Johnny turned to look at his brother, placing his hand on their father's stomach to balance himself. "Dad here is quite the ambitious man, right? Worked hard to achieve the position he has. You think we should peel back another layer?"

"Most certainly. Let's unravel the onion."

"Unravel the onion?" Johnny laughed. "Rotten onion."

"Father, what do you think the board of the Humane Society would do if they were to learn that Joe Santini, their President, beats his wife …"

"I don't …"

Johnny slapped his stomach. "Uh-uh. Don't bother. I've been blind for a long time, but Mickey here has finally brought light back into my world. I will forever hate myself for not having realized it sooner, but I know it's true. You've been beating her for as long as we can remember. The telltale signs were there. I just refused to see them. Not anymore." He slapped his father's stomach again. "So, cut the fuckin' crap."

Their father sagged into the bed. "Fine. You've figured it out."

"What would the Humane Society think of their President dicking around with a bunch of prostitutes?" Johnny asked.

Joe began to respond but Johnny reached over and pinched his lips shut.

"Hold on a sec, before you answer that question, let me take care of a layer for you." He slowly released his father's lips and when Johnny saw that he would remain quiet, he continued. "The piano player. What's her name? Twyla Jones? Interesting thing she told me while she was going down on me. You want to know what it was?"

Their father nodded his head.

"She just turned nineteen last week. I told her 'Happy Birthday.' Later on, we were talking about you and her and the girls. Twyla said she's been coming here for about three years now. Would you like me to do the math for you?" Mickey waited and Joe said nothing. "She was fifteen the first time, Dad."

"Here's what I'm thinking." Mickey took over for his brother. "The publicity of all of this would destroy you. Mom, damaged as she already is, would likely be irretrievably gone forever, and the Humane Society -- once it learned of the beatings, the hookers, and your experience with Twyla – would fire your ass, sue you, and do everything it could to wash the earth of your presence. I'm pretty confident the Humane Society would not treat you very humanely."

"You got any idea what the statute of limitations is on statutory rape?" Johnny asked.

Mickey and Joe shrugged their shoulders. "Does it matter?" Mickey asked.

"Hey, I'm just suggesting there's another layer."

"Fair enough."

"What do you want?" Joe asked. "I know I'd like an ithe pack for my fathe."

Mickey and Johnny began to laugh. "An ithe pack. He'd like an ithe pack," Mickey said, looking at his brother. "Dad, haven't you figured it out yet? There's no help for you from us. There's only what you're going to do to get out of this predicament that you, and only you, have put yourself into."

"Here's the deal." Johnny sat on the far edge of the bed. Mickey sat on the other -- brotherly bookends to their father. "Leave. Now." Mickey said. "Never turn back. Leave your bank book behind. We'll be needing it to get Mom out of jail on Monday and to provide for her in your absence."

"Bank book? What the fuck's a bank book?" Johnny said. "Don't you mean his check book? His credit cards? Cash.? Bank book? What the hell?"

"Johnny, calm down. I believe the man now understands the request if he didn't already. You have more than clarified it for him."

"We go to your boss and to the press," Mickey continued. "We tell them the whole sordid tale and provide them with the check made payable to Ladies For You drawn from your account and cashed by Cecilia no doubt some time today."

"We'll hire a divorce lawyer for Mom and get a restraining order kicking you out of this house," Johnny added. "We'll make sure the lawyer bleeds you dry of everything you own."

"You boyth couldn't afford a lawyer."

"No, we couldn't," Mickey agreed. "That's why he'd have to bleed you like a leech."

"You thertainly make it thound eathy."

"It is. Tell us where everything is. Your bank book, as it were," Johnny said, winking at Mickey. "We gather everything up and leave.

147

Then, you can figure out how to untie yourself and leave. I don't care if you take a fuckin' dirigible and float off to Germany. Just leave. We'll be back in 24 hours. If you're still here, I think Mickey will have something else to say with his fists. Won't you, my pugilistic philosophizing brother?"

"About that. Dad, I'm sorry."

"Shut the fuck up," Johnny screamed at Mickey.

"Dude, I can't help it. I'm sorry."

"Mickey, it'th not too late …" Joe began before Johnny reached out and slapped him hard.

"You, shut the fuck up. One more word from you and you'll be wishing for a spot six feet under to escape the pain I'd inflict on your ass. Maybe buried so far down that you become a part of Earth's features studied by geologist's centuries from now. How about that? Huh?" Johnny slapped him again. "You want to become a part of the magma?"

"Mickey, get him off of me, would ya?"

"Nah, I'm fine."

Silence erupted and filled the room. Outside, a screen door slammed. An engine started. The wind rustled the tree outside the window causing the branches to scratch against the glass pane.

A long sigh ruptured the silence, followed by Joe's words. "The bank book, ath it were, ith …"

"We know where the bank book is. We already wrote a check on it."

"My wallet ith in our bedroom on the drether. Credit cardth, ATM card, a few other thingth are in there."

"That it?" Johnny growled.

"Yeth."

Johnny slapped Joe again. "Try looking at me when you say it."

Silence erupted again in full blown glory. Birds squawked in the tree. A dog barked. A child screamed. Its mother screamed louder.

"There'th a thafe in the clothet. The combination'th 32-18. There'th cath there. Thome thtockth.

Johnny leaned in close as his father tried to pull away. "Was that so hard?" Johnny placed a kiss on Joe's forehead and then rose from the bed. "What do you think, Mickey? Are we missing anything?"

Mickey pondered it for a moment, his chin resting in his chin, shoulders hunched. "Nope. I think that's it. Although I think we need to make sure the dirigible is inflated."

Before Johnny could stop laughing and respond, Joe interjected. "That'th a good one, thon. I'm jutht hoping you'll at leatht leave me my car."

Which they did after Joe told them all his PINs and passwords.

"First stop. The bank." They were in the Torino, the engine rumbling. Johnny pulled a cigarette out of his pack.

"I thought you were going to stop."

"Give me a fucking break. We just thrashed our dad and you want me to quit smoking. All in the same day."

"Correction. I thrashed him. You just added a little extra to it."

"I gotta give you that. Some day we need to analyze what came over you. I just hope karma isn't gonna get you."

Johnny pulled out into the street and began the slow crawl out of the neighborhood. "Man, I'm bushed," Mickey said. "Don't know if it's beating on Dad, dipping into Cecilia, worrying about home, or everything combined, but I am just beat down at the moment." Mickey slumped against the door and closed his eyes.

"I hear ya." Johnny snickered. "Maybe you got a bacteria." In the passenger seat, Mickey snored quietly. "Yeah. A bacteria..."

149

Johnny whistled to himself, turned the radio on, beat out a tune on the steering wheel, but couldn't resist. "Hey," he said, slapping Mickey on the shoulder. "Wake up."

"Whaaa…"

"Wake up." He slapped him again. "We gotta talk."

"Talk? That's all we been doing since last night. Talk." Mickey curled into himself further. "Let me sleep."

"We did a little more than talk, Mickey. Wake the fuck up." Johnny pulled to the side of the road and slammed on the brakes, bring his brother hurtling into the dashboard.

"What the fuck, Johnny."

"We gotta talk."

"Why?" Mickey settled back in his seat and squinted at the sun. "That's weird."

"What?"

"There's like a halo effect to the light. Do you see it?" Mickey pointed. "Little halos around everything where the light reflects."

Johnny looked out the windshield. "No. It's just a typical shitty Saturday morning. Hot and getting hotter. The light is glaring and I lost my fuckin' sunglasses."

Mickey slowly turned his head to face his brother. "What's wrong with you?"

"What's wrong with me? What's wrong with me?" Johnny almost screamed it. "Did you take some idiot pills or something? Damn. Mom's in jail. You broke Dad's face and we sent him packing. Hopefully. You fall asleep like it's just another day in paradise and you want to know what's wrong with me?"

"Poor Johnny."

"No, you don't. I know what's coming. The philosopher king. I'm right, aren't I?"

Mickey smiled and nodded.

"Don't you do it." Johnny grimaced and started the car forward. "I don't need any of your philosophy crap right now."

"I just think it's interesting. You're proving my point. That's all."

"What point?"

"There was a reason Mom didn't want you to know the truth. I told you last night."

"Well how about you enlighten me again. My memory of last night is a little fuzzy at the moment."

"She didn't think you could handle reality because you break down over the littlest of things." Almost to himself, Mickey mumbled, "While ignoring the big things, of course."

"What was that?"

"Nothing." Mickey reached out and turned the radio on. Johnny just as quickly snapped it off. Mickey turned it back on and glared at Johnny. "I need some music."

"Fine. Could you at least find something other than country music? I don't need that whiny crap this morning."

"Here's the deal, Johnny." Mickey fiddled with the radio until he found a classic rock station. "Good enough for you?"

"Yeah."

"The shit has barely begun and you already think the world is over. We didn't break Dad's face. I did, but you're already a nervous Nellie about it. Yeah, Mom's in jail, but we've now got the resources to get her out." Mickey patted his jacket where their father's checkbook was hidden in the inside pocket, along with the $10,000 in cash they got out of his safe. "Yeah, we've got a labyrinth of problems ahead of us. A whole maze of decisions. Go left. Right.

Who the hell knows? But for the first time in a long time, you're caught up with the fullness of our family picture." Mickey began hammering the dashboard with one hand to the slow beat of the song playing on the radio – *The End* by the Doors. "And we got solutions, fuckin' great solutions to the problems. It is most certainly not the end, my brother. It is only the beginning.

"And you're quivering like a baby because of everything that's been going wrong. I got news for you, Johnny, it's been going wrong for a long, long time. Our Dad's a piece of shit. Our Mom's gone slightly mad because of his abuse. And you and I are good-for-nothing losers who eat at the same crappy diner every Friday night and talk like we own the world when we hardly own the clothes we wear."

"Mickey …"

"No, hold on a sec. We're losers, Johnny. Big fat losers. And now you're practically bawling because that fact has slapped you in the face." Mickey rolled his window down and put his hand out, letting it float on the wind resistance that flowed by as they sped down Folsom Boulevard. "You got a choice. Hell, I got a choice. We can continue the regression of our lives. Or we can choose a different way. To actually begin the process of growing up. Progression, if you will."

"Progression? If I will?" Johnny scoffed. "You ever think that life is easier … more enjoyable … where I am?"

"Regressing? No."

"Fuck regression." Johnny made a u-turn and then a quick right.

"What are you doing?"

"Taking you to your house. I'm done with you."

"What about Dad?"

"What about him?"

"We need to go back later to make sure he's left."

152

"Right now, I don't give a damn. I'm just tired of listening to you lord your supposed superiority over me. Regression. Yeah, I'll give you regression."

"Johnny, come on."

"No. I'm serious. I'll pick you up Monday morning. We'll go to court. See what's what and go from there." Johnny sped up and began rhythmically drumming his fingers on the steering wheel. "You wanna go check on Dad, go for it. I'm taking a break."

"Of course. When the going gets tough …"

Johnny screeched the car to a halt in the middle of the road, cars swerved around them, horns blaring. "Get out."

"Johnny."

"Get. Out."

"Johnny. I don't have a car."

"So what."

"I can't go check on Dad if I don't have a way to get there."

"Take a fuckin' taxi." Johnny shrugged his shoulders. "I don't care. I'm done with this. I'm done with you. Until Monday morning."

"We're in the middle of Folsom Boulevard, Johnny. Can you at least pull over?"

"No. Get out."

"Fine." Mickey watched for an opening in the traffic and opened the door and jumped out.

"You know what I'm going to do," Johnny said, leaning towards the passenger door. "I'm gonna go to the diner and see if Ally wants to go out tonight."

He sped away, the tires squealing as Mickey screamed, "Fuuuuuckkk yoooouuuuuu, Johnny!!!!!!" and shook his fist at the Torino.

After a day-long nap that left him groggier than before, Mickey hoofed it over to the diner. "Where's your brother?" Ally asked peering over his shoulder at the parking lot, as he walked in.

"I don't know and don't care."

"Table for one, then."

"Yes."

Mickey slid into a booth and picked up the menu. "Can I get you something to drink?"

"Ummm … what kind of beer do you have?"

"Wow. Really? You been coming here for how long and you don't know about our incredible beer selection?"

Mickey shrugged his shoulders and smiled at her. "I've never had a beer here. I figure the options aren't that good."

"Well, you're right. Coors, Coors Light, Bud, Bud Light, and PBR."

"You're joking."

"Nope. What do you want?"

"I'll take a PBR, but maybe you could get Billy to allot some of his refrigerator space for something better than cheap American shit."

"I'll get right on that, Mickey," Ally replied. "Or maybe not. He doesn't care. Most of his customers don't either. You see, here at Billy's, there's a perfect fusion between Billy and his customers. They want the basics and nothing more and he's more than happy not having to stretch his mind to anything new. The menu hasn't changed in years. Same stuff his old man served before him and as long as his customers keep coming around, as long as they're still alive, Billy ain't gonna change a thing." She began to turn away before turning back to Mickey. "You need a few minutes or you getting the usual."

Mickey's brow furrowed and he fingered the menu. "Let me take a look at the menu."

"Uh-huh."

"Thanks, Ally," he said to her retreating back. Mickey looked out at the parking lot, the sun reflecting off car windshields blinding him into a squint. He was lost there until Ally returned and left the beer in front of him. Mickey took a sip and then a gulp before leafing through the menu.

"So, cheeseburger?" Mickey looked at Ally, her order pad out. "Bacon?" she asked, a hint of impatience lurking behind her words.

"No."

"No?"

"No."

"Okay. What's it gonna be then?" The impatience had bloomed fully now. Her pencil now tapping a furious beat on the pad.

"I don't know."

"I'll give you a few minutes."

Mickey reached out to her, placing his hand on her arm as she started to turn away from his table. "Don't go yet." He wiped at his eyes. "Please."

"I got customers to wait on."

Mickey looked around. In the opposite corner, three teenage girls sucked at their shakes and giggled. Nobody sat at the counter and the other tables were empty. He raised his eyebrows at her.

"Okay, I don't." Ally dropped her order pad on the table and slid in across from Mickey. She looked into the kitchen before reaching out quickly to grab Mickey's beer and swallow half of what was left. "What's going on?"

"Aaaaaaaahhhhhhh," Mickey sighed. "Everything?" He took the beer from Ally and downed the rest. "Everything," he stated and held out the empty glass to her. "Could you get another?"

"Sure." Ally smiled as she rose.

"Make it two. One for you. If Billy sees it, we'll just tell him it's for Johnny when he gets here."

"He coming?"

"I don't know. But Billy will believe it. When have I ever been here without him?"

"Right." The smile on her face grew as she picked up the empty. Mickey watched her as she walked back behind the counter. Imagining her in his arms almost helped relieve the pressure he was feeling. Almost convinced him that something good might happen after all. He watched her return with two pint glasses of copper colored lager, the condensation dripping down the sides.

"Thank you."

"You bet." Ally sipped at hers and looked over the rim of the glass at Mickey, her eyebrows lifting.

"Did you hear what Johnny and I were talking about last night?"

Ally shrugged. "Not really. Just that you two were arguing more than usual. Something about your Mom and Dad." She put down her beer and began to twirl a loose end of her hair. "And something about me. I think you were even going to ask me out." Her hand flopped to the table. "Until you f'in' blew it."

"That's part of it all. You know?"

She leaned forward then putting her chin in the cup of her hand, the other slowly turning the pint glass in circles. "Why don't you tell me about it?"

"My Mom's in jail."

"That sucks."

156

"It's why I needed a rain check last night."

"Sucks for you."

"My Dad has been beating her as long as I can remember."

"That sucks more."

"I think I really like you."

"That su... What?"

"Just seeing if you're paying attention." Mickey dipped his head to drink long from his beer. "But it's true, too."

Ally lifted her chin from the palm of her hand and reached out to gently lay her hand on Mickey's arm. "I know."

"You ..."

"I've known for a long time."

"But, how could you?"

"Mickey." She patted his arm. "Before you ever realized it yourself, I had a gleaning that something might be brewing between us. I've just been waiting."

"Hey! What the hell's going on out there?" Billy slapped his spatula on the counter that ran between the kitchen and the dining area.

"Cut it out, Billy. I'm taking a break."

"The hell you are. You got customers to serve."

"Billy, there ain't nobody here except for those girls." Ally turned to face him and nodded her head at the corner table where the three girls giggled on, oblivious to the attention brought on them.

"Then wipe down the counter." Billy scratched his head. "Or run the mop around."

"Damn it, Billy. I already ran the mop around. Twice. And the counter's so shiny I practically need sun glasses in here." Ally stood up and crossed the aisle to the counter that ran the length of the restaurant. "Just back off and let me take a little break here. Mickey's got some problems."

Billy scratched his head with the corner of the spatula. "Geez, Ally, what about the beer? I could get in trouble for that, you know. You can't drink on the job."

"It's not mine. It's for his brother." She turned and winked at Mickey.

"It's half gone."

"And?"

"Fine. Just hurry it up."

"Thank you." Ally bowed to Billy and blew him a kiss before turning to return to Mickey's table. The first thing she did was finish off the beer. "Aaaaah."

"Get another one," Mickey whispered.

Ally smiled at him and looked back at the kitchen where Billy was busy prepping his gravy for the Saturday night rush that rarely was. "Why not?" Quietly, she snuck over to the tap and filled her glass. Mickey held his out to her which she snatched and re-filled as well. "These are on Billy," she whispered as she slid back into the booth, this time on Mickey's side.

Ally turned to face Mickey and began twirling her hair again. "Where were we?"

"You were telling me about your gleaning."

"My gleaning?"

"Yeah. You're ..."

"Oh, that's right." She leaned close to Mickey. "I kind of like you and I think you like me. Let's forget about the rain check and last night." Ally took a sip of beer, the moisture left behind glistening on her upper lip. "What do you think?"

"OK. But there's one more thing about last night I think I should tell you about."

Ally rolled her eyes and pulled away. "Please don't."

"You see ... my dad had these hookers at his house."

"No. Really. Don't. You do know that honesty isn't always the best policy?"

Ally and Mickey were interrupted by the screech of brakes in the parking lot. They looked up and saw the Torino parked across two spaces and Johnny hurrying up to the diner's entrance. "I can't believe it," Mickey said, nudging Ally on the shoulder to get her out of his way. He slid across the seat and rose to meet Johnny. "You're actually doing it, aren't you?"

"What the hell are you talking about?"

"You ... you ... you said you were coming here tonight to ask Ally out even though we had a ... you made a brother's promise." Mickey's shoulders slumped. "I can't believe after everything that's happened, you would violate the code."

"You were going to ask me out?"

"Yes ... I mean, no." Johnny wiped sweat off his face and Mickey noticed his bloodshot eyes.

"That sucks."

"Mickey, I wasn't gonna do that. I was just pissed at you." Johnny wrapped his arm around Mickey's shoulder. "Come on. I wouldn't have done that to you. Let's sit down. I've got bad news."

"This for me?" Johnny asked as he took a sip from Ally's beer. "Damn. Beer at Billy's Diner. What have we been doing all this time, Mickey? Coffee and sodas?" He rolled a mouthful of beer around. "PBR. Right?"

"Yes." Ally and Mickey replied in unison.

"Why don't you get yourself one, too, Ally? Join us."

159

"I ... I ..." Ally didn't finish her reply before turning and filling a third pint glass and sliding in next to Mickey, who looked at her with a frown that suggested the questions that lurked in his head. He slipped an inch or two closer to her.

"You mentioned bad news. What's going on?" Mickey asked.

Johnny drained the remains of the beer in the glass in front of him and slammed it down. "Could you get me another?" Ally began to protest. "Please."

"Fine," she snorted before plucking his glass from the table and filling it at the tap. "You two just better be glad it's slow for a Saturday night."

Johnny drained that beer and slammed the glass down. "You see, I ..." Before he could go on, he covered his face with his hands and when he pulled them away a few seconds later, tears were flowing freely down his cheeks. "I ..."

"Johnny? What is it?" Mickey reached his hand out to his brother. "Is it Dad? Did he do something? That fucking asshole. I shoulda killed him last night."

"No ... no ... it's not ... Dad." Johnny drew deep breaths in and out to try to regain control.

"Mom?"

Johnny nodded his head.

"Oh no, I knew leaving her in there for the weekend wasn't a good idea. What happened?" Mickey's hand gripped Johnny's arm tighter. "What? Did somebody beat her up? What, Johnny? What happened?"

He shook his head. "Nobody beat her up."

"That's a fucking relief." Mickey frowned again. "Then what?"

"She ... she ..." Johnny drew in a deep shuddering breath and let it out hard and fast. "She had a heart attack."

"When?"

"When? What does it fucking matter, Mickey? Last night."

"But she's OK, right."

Johnny looked at Mickey and began to shake his head. "No. She's not."

"What do you mean?"

"Mickey. Mom's dead."

Where This Came From: One of the story ideas I had ever since I started writing was a story told entirely in dialogue (or at least almost entirely). Another story idea was to have two guys sitting and talking to each other. So, I started writing this story melding the two together. To add to the dynamic, every few hundred words, I picked a word from the dictionary that I had to use in the next few hundred words. The first word I picked was deviation, hence the title and the overall sense of the story. Originally published for that big book retailer only, I'm including it here so that it's in old-fashioned print as well.

Your lips, soft and warm and moist. They whispered against my skin. I brushed them with my own. They opened and formed words that lifted me to the stars and beyond.

Your eyes, sparkling and opening me to your depths. I could have fallen in and been happy forever.

Your hips that curved.

Your neck that beckoned.

Your fit, perfectly within.

Your arms around me.

Your hands in mine.

Your breasts pressed against me.

Your warmth.

Your smile.

Your laugh.

Your tears.

You.

These parts.

I touched them once. I'll never touch them again. But they will remain with me forever, in my heart, in my soul, wherever I go. These parts.

ACKNOWLEDGEMENTS

Thank you to all the websites that post writing prompts and to the ladies of the Monday evening prompt group I joined a couple of years ago. A lot of these stories are the result of prompts found here and there and a couple of the stories are directly the result of that Monday Evening group. Sometimes the story ideas dry up and the right prompt at the right moment can do wonders.

Thank you also to all of the writers and other creative types I have got to know over the years I've been doing this thing. Audrey, Berthold, Richard, Chuck, and Lucinda at Writers Supporting Writers, for our conservations about writing. And all of the others I've got to know through blogging and Twitter. The conversations about writing, the support we share for each other's efforts, go a long way towards keeping me going at this craft. I'd like to name you all, but that would be impossible. So, I won't try. Just know that I appreciate you.

163

CPSIA information can be obtained
at www.ICGtesting.com
Printed in the USA
BVHW042208260922
648069BV00003B/23